THE HANDSOME
FARMHOUSE GHOST

Tina Griffith

Order this book online at www.trafford.com
or email orders@trafford.com

Most Trafford titles are also available at major online book retailers.

Cover designed by
Nicole Hartl

Printed in the United States of America.

ISBN: 978-1-4269-3772-9 (sc)
ISBN: 978-1-4269-3773-6 (e-book)

Library of Congress Control Number: 2010911500

*Our mission is to efficiently provide the world's finest, most comprehensive
book publishing service, enabling every author to experience success.
To find out how to publish your book, your way, and have it available
worldwide, visit us online at www.trafford.com*

Trafford rev. 9/17/2010

www.trafford.com

North America & international
toll-free: 1 888 232 4444 (USA & Canada)
phone: 250 383 6864 ♦ fax: 812 355 4082

When I want you in my arms
When I want you and all your charms
Whenever I want you all I have to do is dream

When I feel blue in the night
And I need you to hold me tight
Whenever I want you all I have to do is
Dre-e-e-e-m

I can make you mine, taste your lips of wine ♫
Anytime night or day
Only trouble is, gee whiz
I'm dreamin' my life away

I need you so, that I could cry
I love you so, and that is why
♪ Whenever I want you all I have to do is

&ö DREAM cз

CHAPTER ONE

Knock, knock, knock!

Abby, busy cooking in the kitchen and oblivious to the rest of the world, whipped around when she heard the strong knock on her front door. She moved the hot pot to the cold burner and wiped her hands on the tea towel as she moved away from the stove. She wasn't expecting anyone but walked quickly to the front door, thinking that it might be her fiancé, Casey, surprising her by coming home a day early.

Abby pulled the door open and then hastily took a few steps backwards. Instantly, her fashionable smile turned into a blank stare.

Abby gasped loudly when she saw two fully uniformed police officers standing on her porch, their rigid hats being removed from their heads.

"Are you Abigail Elexus Hudson?" asked the tall, darker haired official-looking man. Both officers pulled out their badges so that Abby could see their I.D's.

Abby was dumb-founded and speechless. She nodded slightly but had no idea what to do next. She kept looking back and forth at both their faces, waiting for one of them to announce what they wanted from her. Surely it couldn't be anything serious, she speculated.

Abby needed to calm down. Her silly mind was just jumping to conclusions. Maybe they were about to ask for a donation to their next policeman's ball, she pondered in a moment of jest. Then she scolded herself for watching too many movies.

The taller officer took a step backwards.

Abby watched as the other cop, a slightly shorter man, shed

a tiny tear from his left eye. It was almost undetectable, and could have gone unnoticed, except that he brought his hand up to wipe the small drop away.

Abby's breathing almost stopped as she realized that something was dreadfully wrong, only she wasn't sure what it could be. The shorter officer leaned in and finally spoke his first words. "May we come inside for a quick moment?"

Abby felt paralyzed. Suddenly, she became aware that this may not be a joke. "Of course", she breathed. She moved aside and let them pass through the tiny doorway. She watched as they stood in the middle of her living room, feet slightly apart, hats in their hands and brought down to a V-formation below their belly.

"You may want to have a seat", suggested the shorter officer, Gary Winslow.

Officer Winslow's own body and soul was fighting between the reality which is now his life, and his duty as a cop. He knew that he needed to be professional so that he could help this woman with her own tragedy, but his emotions were getting the better of him.

Officer Winslow had lost his brother, Tyson, four weeks ago in a traffic accident and was still highly traumatized by the whole thing. He had just returned back to work nine days ago after making himself a promise that he would only grieve for his brother when he was alone. He was told by his captain to take all the time off that he needed, but he felt it was better to be at work, surrounded by people and things to do, than to be at home and suffer alone.

With his brother's face in the forefront of his thoughts, his sad brown eyes shifted upwards to the lovely woman's face as he forced his mind to focus on the task at hand. "We're here with bad news about your friend, Casey."

With the impromptu mention of her fiancé's name, Abby felt like the air had been violently sucked out of her lungs. She took a step backwards and slumped heavily into the nearby easy chair. Her body was going numb, her eyes were losing focus, and her skin was growing colder by the second. Every part of her body was screaming, "No, no, no!" while nothing escaped from her lips.

The two officers looked towards each other, not knowing which one was going to offer the bad news. When it wasn't being delivered, Officer Winslow, the senior of the two, spoke up.

"A small West Jet plane crashed three minutes after take-off from the Fort Myers Southwest Florida Airport on November 29", he began. "The flight was bound for LAX in Los Angeles, California - an approximate eight hour flight. Sadly, all people onboard were killed."

Abby felt herself being drawn into a very deep, dark hole.

The last time she spoke with Casey was in the evening on November 28. He said that he had landed okay, the weather seemed fine, and he would call her again in a few days.

Casey went on to say that he would be tied up with meetings from 8 to 4pm every day, and he will be trying to get caught up on his paper work from 5 to 10 every night. "I will call you the night before I leave, so don't you worry your pretty head about nothing, darlin'."

Both officers watched as Abby looked like she was going into shock. Officer Winslow's face came closer to hers and his voice softened. "I'm sorry to have to tell you this, but we believe that Casey was one of those people."

Without looking down, Abby felt the fingers of her right hand fly to the ring finger on her left hand and lovingly caress the engagement ring that her beloved had put on her just a few weeks ago. Instantly, it made her feel closer to the man that she wanted to marry.

Officer Winslow watched as the woman before him fell apart and his heart went out to her. He could no longer speak as his own voice was beginning to crack. He was starting to relive the moment when he had found out about his only brother being killed, and this was not okay while he was on duty.

The officer swallowed hard and took a step backwards, hoping that his partner would take over the rest of the conversation.

Abby was having a very hard time processing the information that she had just been given. Why would he be going to California, she wondered as the tears streamed down her face. This didn't make any sense. Casey was in Florida for the week on business. Had anything happened to him, surely someone would have called her before now.

Disbelief turned to anguish. "This can't be real", she cried out loud to no one in particular. A very distraught Abby bent forward and cried into the palms of her open hands. She found this situation very hard to understand.

Abby's red and puffy face looked up to the other officer and waited. "This has got to be some kind of a mistake", she announced, hoping that he would give her a different story. "The plane couldn't have crashed. Maybe you have the wrong Casey Katan. My Casey is a computer analyst for Bentall Management. They have offices and factories all around the world that need attention or servicing. Casey goes out of town at least once a month and nothing has ever happened before."

Abby could feel her face go flush and her heart start beating stronger within her chest as she waited for his reply. Her head went dizzy and she was glad that she was sitting down.

Officer Nicholas Gatling, who had been mostly quiet up until now, came forward to deliver the rest of the intricate information. He knew about Officer Winslow's personal life and could see that his partner needed a minute or two to compose himself.

Officer Gatling came and knelt down beside Abby, placing one of his hands on top of hers in a fatherly fashion as he spoke. His voice was full of tenderness and compassion while he tried to give the best explanation that he could.

"There are many different reasons why a plane crash may occur", he began.

Abby tried to hear the words as he continued to speak, but it confused her even more. Too much was being thrown at her all at once. She felt as if she was beginning to suffocate with information.

Officer Gatling used both hands to list the reasons of which he referred to, extending a different finger for each one.

"Piloting errors, faulty equipment, violations of FAA regulations, design or structural problems, flight service negligence, air traffic controller error, fueling error, and the list goes on."

He took a second and watched as Abby's expression went blank. Officer Nicholas Gatling could feel the terror and confusion run through her body because of the words that he had just delivered.

The handsome, 29-year old cop was a strong and protective individual with a good heart and a level head. He was extremely sensitive because he was raised by a single mom and four older sisters who taught him all about women's feelings.

The man under the uniform wanted to hold this beautiful woman in his arms and make everything okay, but he was on duty. Knowing this, Officer Gatling lowered his gaze and tried to gain back his focus.

The sad cop began again, only this time he was more formal. "Federal, state, and agency laws govern the activities of most aircrafts. However, strict adherence to these rules and regulations may not always be the case.

Abby tried to hear his words but found it all to be quite gibberish. The strong beat of her heart was pounding in her ears, her mouth was desperately dry, and she could feel her body wanting to crumble to the ground in a giant heap. She was dealing with a tornado of emotions that was crippling her from the inside out. It was all she could do to try to hear the words that were being said, without completely fainting away.

Officer Gatling watched as the beautiful woman was trying so hard to understand. He could see that she didn't, and Officer Gatling knew what he was doing to her, yet he felt he should continue. How he hated his job sometimes.

"Not following the mandated guidelines is a prime recipe for aviation disaster", he said with a bit of anger. Secretly he was venting over the fact that his father had died in a plane crash because the pilot had not checked all of his equipment or controls properly before take-off.

Realizing that his voice had become hard, he took a deep breath and shook the memory out of his mind. He looked right into Abby's beautiful and tearful eyes and continued in a softer tone.

"Even in cases where negligence is not the primary cause of an aviation emergency, natural causes such as weather could also play a major role in an airplane disaster."

Again he stopped talking to watch Abby's expression. Seeing the pain on her face, reminded him of the day when his mother was told about her husband's death. It made the man under the uniform suffer relentlessly as he watched this beautiful girl's mind explode into a thousand pieces, just as it had done to his mother.

Officer Gatling could see from her expression that he wasn't getting through to her. He finally leaned forward and placed a loving hand on her shoulder, while his own heart was starting to break. "I'm terribly sorry for you", he stated sincerely while slowly moving his soft hand up and down her arm from her shoulder to her elbow. "I think I've said enough for now."

He hated the almost monthly phrase that he had to extend to one person or another when someone they know had died. Today's speech was no exception, but it somehow hurt the most.

Officer Winslow had been sitting back and listening to the entire conversation, his own turmoil at bay for the moment. He saw the look on the faces of the other two people in the room and he could feel the propensity building on both sides. He could see that things were now starting to take another route, and he became concerned.

Abby was emotional and needed consoling. Officer Gatling was sympathic and looked like he might want to oblige.

Sensing that something was about to happen between them, Office Winslow stood up. He knew that he needed to get his partner out of the house and away from this girl before she asked them to stay. Because he knew what this woman was going through, he felt horrible with himself for what he was about to do, but he needed to act as a cop.

Officer Winslow walked over and gently punched his partner's shoulder before he piped up. "Miss Hudson", he whispered softly. "Thank you for your time. Let us know if there's anything more we can do for you." He put his hand into the front pocket of his shirt and laid a business card on the nearby table within her reach. He then waved her his good-bye while extending his sympathies about Casey.

The nudge on the shoulder snapped Officer Gatling out of the spell that he was in and he quickly came back to reality. He looked up and into his buddy's eyes as he heard him speak. Officer Gatling wasn't sure if he should thank his partner, or scold him for turning him away from Abby's attention. After a mere second, he decided that his partner was right.

Office Gatling sadly turned and looked back into Abby's soft, brown eyes and then he stood up. He dejectedly made a firm decision to do his job as a cop. His duty that day was done and it was now time to move on. "I'm so sorry for your loss", he stated sincerely as he started walking away from her.

Abby watched as the two officers slowly maneuvered themselves to the front door. She couldn't believe that they were going to just walk away, leaving her to deal with this situation on her own.

Her eyes became as big as saucers as she braced herself on the large arms of the chair that she was sitting in. When they left, she knew that she was going to be alone, terrified, and quite vulnerable. She would need comforting as this moment was too large for her to deal with on her own. Could she not get comfort from them, she wondered. Would they not stay until she felt better?

The officers stopped and turned around before they secured a step outside, and took one last look at Abby. They could see how much hurt they had bestowed upon her and both were dreadfully sorry.

With one hand on the door knob, Officer Winslow paused. His heart was in his throat and he hated leaving her, but he knew that he had to. He patiently waited until their eyes met and then he instantly recognized the pain that she was feeling. He knew with his whole heart that it would not measure what she would feel the next day when it really hit her.

Abby then looked across the room and into Officer Gatling's almond-shaped brown eyes and desperately wished for him to stay. The salty tears that were teasing to come out of her, were being held back in case the kind officer agreed to keep her company.

The moment and choice nearly killed him, but Officer Gatling knew that he couldn't linger. The beautiful woman before him needed time to heal. In his mind he wished her well. Then he smiled politely and gracefully exited her home.

When Abby saw them leave, she couldn't believe it. The door closed and she immediately crumbled into a dark abyss. She fell to the floor in a crying heap, not believing the entire scenario and hoping that this was a nightmare that would end very quickly. "No!" she screamed again and again, only this time out loud for the whole world to hear. "No-o-o-o-o-o!"

Officer Winslow scolded himself because he knew how much she hurt and how quickly he himself could drop into a deep despair. For his own piece of mind, he had to block out her haunting outcry of pain and keep putting one foot in front of the other, knowing that there was nothing he could do to help her.

Officer Winslow walked beside his partner, matching his quick pace step-by-step. He turned and noticed how badly his fellow officer was feeling by the way Officer Gatling looked towards the ground as they walked, instead of towards the car. He'd never done that before. "You okay, man?" Officer Winslow asked while placing a gentle hand on his partner's shoulder.

Without looking up or changing the speed of his pace, Officer Gatling nodded slightly but his head was still hanging forward. He could hear Abby's screams and he wanted to rush back to her side, but he knew better.

Officer Gatling felt sorry for Abby. She was a pretty young thing and didn't deserve to have her heart broken as badly as this. He hoped that she would have a speedy recovery. Maybe he'd even look in on her in a few days.

Officer Nick Gatling had to put her out of his mind. He raised his chin and firmly placed his hat on his head to remind himself that he was a cop first and a man second.

Officer Winslow saw the slight change in his partner's spirit and patted his fellow officer's back. "Good man", was all he said.

Officer Gatling took a quick look towards Abby's home as he started the car. He secretly wished her well, shifted the vehicle into gear, and the two policemen drove off.

CHAPTER TWO

Abby rolled the elegant engagement ring around and around her finger, and sobbed uncontrollably while feeling totally destroyed inside. Her whole world had changed and she wasn't sure what to do next. She had never felt this alone before.

Abby's mind suddenly popped with an answer. "Mom!" she shouted. She pulled herself up from the large chair and ran to the phone. She then dialed her mother's number, which was answered on the second ring.

"Hello, my darling Abby."

After hearing her mother's familiar voice for even that one second, Abby immediately felt better. Abby started talking and told her mom about Casey and the plane crash.

Elizabeth Hudson, Abby's mother, was leveled by the news. "Are you sure, dear?" she asked in total surprise with panic in her voice.

"I'm afraid I am, mom."

Elizabeth trembled as she pressed her ear very closely to the receiver and listened painstakingly as her daughter recited everything that the officers had told her.

"Oh dear", she whispered into the phone. "My poor baby."

Once Abby had finished apprising her mother of the information that had ripped out her heart, she began to cry again.

"I'll be right over."

"Thanks, mom."

The conversation was now done and Abby went upstairs

to run a hot bath. When the water reached the maximum level of height and warmth, Abby came down to the kitchen. After pouring herself a tall, strong drink of rum and coke, Abby went back up and slipped into the very warm bath where she cried for the next little while.

Elizabeth Hudson, a tall and beautiful, well-preserved, 49-year old widow for a year, broke down and cried after she hung up from her youngest daughter. Elizabeth knew first-hand how the burst of unexpected grief feels and did not want that for her child.

After collecting herself, Elizabeth dashed to her computer and found the information pertaining to the crash all over the internet. "Oh, my!" she cried as her hand flew to her mouth. She read as much as she needed and then left her home. She then raced against the clock to be by her daughter's side.

The hot bath did a world of good for Abby. She sobbed quietly as she thought about how things were now, and wondered how they were going to be in the future. After a while, the water in the tub turned cold and she decided to get out. She toweled herself off and then sat on the edge of the bed, wondering what to do next.

With the front door unlocked but closed against the hinges, Abby's mom let herself in and found her young daughter sitting on the edge of her bed, pale and in an almost zombie-like state. "My poor baby", she cooed while walking across the padded floor. She hated seeing her daughter like that.

Abby looked up to see her beloved mother coming into her bedroom. "Oh mom!" she moaned, bursting into more tears. She reached out her arms to her only living parent, who immediately returned the embrace. Abby was thrilled to see her. She suddenly felt like a toddler who had lost her favorite stuffed bear and her mother had found it and brought it back to her.

After placing herself slowly down on the bed, Elizabeth hugged Abby and each cried for their own reasons.

"We'll get through this", Elizabeth whispered as she laid her cheek against Abby's dark hair. "It's going to be all right." Of course, Elizabeth knew that her daughter had a hard road ahead of her, but she also knew that Abby would make it.

Elizabeth's own feelings of grief were very raw due to the fact that she was still reeling with the pain of losing her husband a short year ago. She knew that she now had to put her own emotions aside and pull all of her strength together to help her young daughter in this horrible moment.

Mother and daughter stayed sitting on the edge of the bed for another little while before Elizabeth insisted that Abby get up and dressed for dinner. Elizabeth, in the meantime, went down to the kitchen and fixed up a meal that she knew was a favorite from Abby's childhood.

Abby didn't want to move, but did so on her mother's gentle orders. As she unhurriedly moved about her bedroom, she could hear her mother banging softly in the kitchen below her room.

Seven minutes later, Elizabeth watched the smile grow on Abby's face as she came downstairs and walked towards the table. Her brown eyes widen with joy once she saw the deliciously grilled, double-cheese sandwiches and steaming tomato with rice soup before her.

Abby ran over and hugged her mother with both arms. "Thanks, mom. You always know how to make things better."

Elizabeth tenderly patted her daughter's back in appreciation for her love.

They finished their embrace and then sat down to eat. No words were spoken, but small moans of gratification could be heard after every bite.

After a short while, Elizabeth sensed that Abby needed her close by, so when they were finished their meal she called her work and arranged for some time off. She explained the situation to her superior and was pleased when her boss said yes.

Abby and Elizabeth slept in the same bed that night, for the first time since Abby was little. Each needed the other and both felt better by morning.

The next day, and with her daughter's consent and encouragement, Elizabeth brought a few things from her home to Abby's. She made a space for herself in the second bedroom, which was being used as a computer room. The red futon was pulled out and made into a bed, and the computer desk was pushed to the other wall.

Elizabeth brought her own pillows and a comforter from her home to make herself more content. At bedtime, the girls made sure that the bedroom doors stayed open so that the two women could talk from across the hall until they both fell asleep.

"Night, mom."

"Good night, my darling daughter."

The next morning to mid-afternoon, they talked about

and arranged a small, private memorial service for Casey at the nearby church. Elizabeth took the responsibility of calling people with the news. A week later, fifteen people showed up at the tiny chapel, wishing Abby well and hoping that her pain would not last.

Abby walked a few feet inside the tiny chapel and froze. While she loved the structural building and all it had to offer, she was blown away by the reason that she was there. The faint, somber church music was playing off in the distance and the air had a heavy quality to it.

Once inside, Abby saw a few people that she'd met while being with Casey, and a few friends that she had before her life with him. All of them ran up to comfort her when they saw her, offering Abby their condolences and giving her hugs of strength. Soon, the mournful music began to get louder, which signaled the beginning of the memorial service. They stopped talking and everyone went inside to find a seat.

The service lasted an hour but Abby didn't hear a word of what was being said. Abby's heart was wishing that he was still here with her. Her tearful eyes were focused solely on the mesmerizing 10"x12" framed picture of Casey, which sat near the front of the small hall. The photo was surrounded by a dozen lit white candles and one bouquet after another of beautifully arranged flowers.

Once the service was complete, the minister came and offered a single red rose to Abby's hands. Without thinking, she reached up and took it. The well-kempt, formally-dressed man then gave her his own condolences for her loss. Abby thanked him and then placed the flower closer to her chest and kept it there until they were told to stand for the final prayer.

When the service was done, Elizabeth escorted her daughter outside where both enjoyed the fresh, open air. The minister came to their side and wished them both well in the future. As the others came and said their good-byes, Abby concluded that it was great seeing everyone again, even under such dire circumstances.

Driving away, Abby felt even more remorse than before. It felt like the end of the story and she wasn't even half-way through the book yet. She cried as her mother drove her back home, her mind scattered with one memory after another of her unfinished life with Casey Katan.

Abby went straight to bed once they arrived back at her home. She covered herself up with a thick, colorful quilt, and stayed there for the next few hours.

Elizabeth made herself comfortable on the couch and tried to watch TV as she listened to her daughter's sobbing. She felt useless and unproductive but knew that she needed to stay close just in case Abby called for her.

Abby stayed in bed for the next week and a half. She didn't want to eat, talk, or walk around. She let her mother fuss over her and she liked it. During that time they talked, they cried, and they worked through some of the pain.

Elizabeth tried everything in her power to help her daughter feel better, but she knew that this was something that Abby would eventually have to handle by herself.

Abby felt horrible for three weeks in total. Except for the memorial service, she couldn't get out of bed for two, couldn't eat for one, and pledged that she would not smile forever.

People were phoning Abby's home but she wasn't answering or returning any calls. Abby wanted to die but didn't have the strength. She just wanted her life back to the way it was before. She wanted Casey home again. Nothing else made sense.

At the end of week three, Elizabeth felt very guilty about her work. She knew that it was time for her to go back, but she struggled emotionally as she also wanted to stay with her daughter.

"You go, mom", Abby insisted bravely as she clutched the blanket tighter around her body. She made herself comfortable on the couch while she spoke thoughtfully to her mother. "I'll be okay."

Abby grasped the idea that she will not be okay for a while, but she also acknowledged that it was time for her to carry on with her life again.

"If you're sure." Elizabeth was thrilled that her daughter was trying to be so brave. They hugged and held onto each other for a full minute.

Elizabeth left Abby's home and was back at work within 48 hours. She trusted her heart that Abby would be okay, but she still called her daughter every other hour of every single day.

Abby hated being alone again, but knew that her mother was right.

CHAPTER THREE

Chapter Three

While Abby stayed indoors, moping about and trying to make sense of her life, Elizabeth was between work and home thinking long and hard on how to make her daughter's life better.

After stewing about it for a few days, she finally had an exciting idea that she thought would give her daughter a bit of hope, and she couldn't wait to share it. The idea was so brilliant, that instead of reaching Abby by phone, Elizabeth rushed over to her daughter's home that very afternoon.

While driving down the highway at top speed, Elizabeth realized the irony of the moment: The day was four weeks since Abby got told of Casey's death. Hopefully the good news will outweigh the date.

Abby was watching TV, wrapped in a fuzzy blanket sitting on the couch, when she heard a car pull up outside of her home. She sat up to see her mom getting out of the blue Toyota and then she saw her rushing to get to Abby's front door.

Elizabeth came in smiling to beat the band. "How are you doing, sweetheart?" she asked as she breezed passed her daughter. She didn't wait for a reply as she was on a mission. "Don't get up. I'll be right back." She waved her hand in the air as a gesture for Abby to stay put.

Abby watched as her mom rushed past her and went into the kitchen to make tea and toast for the two of them. She then came back into the living room and sat down beside her young daughter.

"My darling girl", she commented when she saw the surprised look on Abby's face. She moved her forehead closer and closer until it touched. "How are you?"

"I'm okay", she sighed. She touched foreheads with her mom and it made her smile. Abby was very happy to have her mom back in her home again, but wondered why it seemed like she had something up her sleeve.

"Good, let's eat!"

Elizabeth stroked Abby's hair and watched as her daughter gained a bit of strength from the food. She marveled at how much Abby looked like her dad: The large dark eyes, the shiny black hair, and the slightly darker complexion. Abby had the smaller frame of her mother's side of the family, but she got everything else from her father.

Elizabeth got a bit choked up thinking about her late husband and how much their daughter resembled him. She cringed when she remembered his last day on Earth. In the morning he was fine. Later in the day he was gone forever. No-one saw it coming.

Henry was in the backyard cutting the grass and pulling the weeds. Elizabeth went to the window and was about to call him for lunch when she suddenly stopped to stare. She put both elbows up on the window sill and propped up her head as she swooned in his direction. She admired his slightly-graying, curly, dark hair, his strong and weathered hands, his lean body, and his wide shoulders. She loved his strength, his quiet manner, and the way he adored her.

Henry felt someone watching him so he looked towards the house. He saw his lovely wife spying on him through the kitchen window and it moved him. He loved her as much in that moment as he did when they shared their first kiss.

Henry smiled brightly and winked in her direction. He hoped that she knew how much he truly loved and appreciated her.

As their eyes met and he gave her that special look, Elizabeth sighed. After 32 years of married life, she was still so much in love with her handsome and brilliant school-teacher husband.

Elizabeth watched Henry doing his thing for another minute or two. When she felt the time was getting past her, she called his name out the kitchen window and asked him if he wanted something to eat. It was almost lunchtime and she knew that he hadn't eaten for a few hours.

Henry stood up when he heard his wife calling. He straightened his back while holding one hand over his left hip and looked around the yard. He still had a bit of work to do but decided that he would indeed take a short break. "Yeah, okay", he replied as he slapped his hands together.

Henry took one step forward and his head went light. His right hand flew up to his forehead and his eyes began to flutter. It took a minute between him losing his balance and then falling hard to the ground.

Elizabeth watched him go down and screamed out his name. She bolted from the house and knelt by his side. "Henry!" she kept screaming. His eyes were closed and it didn't look like he was breathing.

Elizabeth pushed on his body, rocking it from side to side, but he wasn't moving or responding. She ran back to the house and grabbed the portable phone. She dialed 9-1-1 with her thumb as she sprinted back to the man she loved.

The ambulance came in eight minutes and then the paramedics tried to help him. After realizing the seriousness of his condition, they rushed him to the nearest hospital. The hospital staff worked on him for what seemed like an eternity while Elizabeth waited in the small corridor.

The doctor in charge finally came out and walked towards the terrified woman. He held both of her hands as he told Elizabeth that Henry had suffered an embolism. "He was gone before the ambulance reached the hospital and there was nothing that anyone could do to bring him back", he said as kindly as he could.

"No-o-o-o-o-o-o-o!" she shouted with fear in her heart and agony in her soul.

The doctor kept saying how sorry he was for her loss but Elizabeth was already on her knees, screaming and crying for Henry to come back. Her life with him wasn't done yet. They were supposed to grow old together.

Two nurses and an intern heard the commotion from another room and came running out. They saw what was happening and ran to the doctor's aid. Together they helped a very distraught Elizabeth to a quiet room and tried to comfort her until her two daughters took her home.

Elizabeth remembered how she felt that day when the doctor told her that Henry was gone. She didn't think she would ever get over that horrible moment and she wanted to die to be with him.

Elizabeth knew first-hand the intense emotional pain that one feels from losing your other half, and she wanted to help her daughter get through her dreadful situation.

Elizabeth sat up straight and cleared her throat. She removed the small tears that had escaped from her eyes as she went back in time. She then turned and looked into her daughter's perfectly-shaped face. "I have something for you", she announced.

Abby couldn't imagine what it could be. She watched her mother pull something out of her large purse.

Elizabeth turned and presented a rather official-looking document to Abby, as well as something that looked like a money order.

Abby didn't know what to say. As she checked it over, she inhaled quickly and turned to gaze into her mother's watery eyes.

"This, my dear daughter, is the deed to a farm that I inherited from my uncle many years ago, plus a small fortune of $20,000 to keep you going for a while.

"Oh, mom!" Abby exclaimed as she shifted around in her spot on the couch. She stared at her mom in disbelief. "You can't just give this away. It means so much to you."

"And you mean more", Elizabeth said as she leaned in to hug her tearful daughter. "Get away for a while and find your smile. You never know what else you may find out there."

Elizabeth suddenly called to mind all the times when she had visited the old farmhouse as a young girl. The silly adventures, the tea-parties under the tree, and the scary sleep-overs where all the kids thought they heard ghosts in the attic, gave her a life-time of wonderful memories. She smiled to herself as she remembered all those happy moments.

Elizabeth had every intention to move to the farmhouse herself when she and her husband retired, but God had other plans. Without Henry in her life, it just wouldn't be the same now.

"I can't believe this", she sighed. Abby beamed at how thoughtful her mother was to her, and then looked around the room that they were sitting in. She took stock of all the things that she had gained in the last year or two of her life. These were bought with Casey by her side.

Although Abby had not been to the farmhouse in a very long time, she remembered it to be a small building. She knew that she couldn't possibly take everything with her, but how could she part with some of these precious treasures?

The idea of leaving their items behind, brought tears to Abby's eyes. She wasn't sure that vacating her home was the right thing to do, but she knew that her mother had never been wrong before.

Abby locked eyes with her only living parent and smiled her deep appreciation. She knew in her heart that as much as she didn't believe it at the moment, everything would eventually be okay. "Thanks mom."

"You're very welcome, my darling little girl." They talked for another little while, and then said their good-byes.

As she waved to the moving car, Abby decided that her mother was right. She needed a new start, but hesitated. "I can't do this alone", she complained. "Who can I get to come with me? Who is adventurous enough to want to go with me?"

A tiny set of lines creased across her almost perfect forehead, and then it hit her. "Melissa!" she screamed. She ran to the phone and pressed the number four redial key, then sat back and waited for her older sister to answer. Her heart started pumping with anticipation as this would be the first time in three weeks since the two girls had spoken.

Melissa Hudson, taller with more defined details, was the total opposite of Abby. Melissa looked more like her mother's side of the family – the eyes, hair, and the shape of her face. Put the two girls in the same room and you couldn't tell that they were related.

"Hello?" came the familiar female voice.

Abby and Melissa were not only sisters, but used to be the best of friends while growing up. When Casey came into the picture, that ended. Neither one liked the other which made things difficult for Abby. Where once the sisters were so close, they now only talked about once a month.

"Hi Melissa, it's me, Abby."

After exchanging pleasantries, Abby wondered if Melissa knew that Casey had passed away. "I guess you've heard about Casey?" she asked boldly.

Melissa heard about Casey's death through their mom. Elizabeth had called all the family members and friends of Abby and Casey a few weeks ago, to inform them of his passing and when and where the memorial service would be held.

Melissa had only met with him a few times so she didn't go to the church. There was something about Casey that Melissa didn't like, so they never became friends. At best, she tolerated the man because of her sister.

Melissa bowed her head and sighed heavily. "I did and I'm so sorry", she said. "I left you a message a few weeks ago after mom called me, but I guess you didn't get it yet."

Abby interrupted with embarrassment. "I probably got

it", she agreed once she remembered the flashing red light on her phone. "I just haven't checked my phone messages yet."

Melissa phoned Abby and left a short message of condolence when she found out, but it was not with sadness for him. It was with sadness for her sister and how she would be feeling.

"No worries", she began sweetly. "I think you have had enough on your plate these past few weeks."

"Thank you for understanding. Now, how are you, sis?"

The two girls talked for the next hour and got all caught up with their news. Abby told Melissa about their mom giving her the farmhouse and then asked if she wanted to check it out with her.

Abby heard her sister gasp into the receiver.

"Are you kidding?" Melissa yelled into the phone. Remembering those times as children when they visited the farmhouse, brought her sheer joy. "When are you planning to go?"

"I'm not sure. How about tomorrow or the day after that?" Secretly, she hoped that it would be sooner rather than later.

Melissa had to think of what she was doing over the next day or two, but knew she would cancel whatever it was to be able to see the old farmhouse again. "I think that could be arranged", Melissa snickered with delight. She couldn't wait to get started.

"And there's no offense or bad feelings because mom gave me the deed to the farmhouse and not you?" she questioned, hoping this would not come between them.

Melissa knew that Abby would live there for a while because of her immediate situation, but it would always belong to the both of them. "No, none at all", she laughed.

Abby was quite relieved. "Thank goodness." A smile appeared on Abby's youthful face and her eyes twinkled with happiness at the prospect of seeing her sister again.

Once she was filled in on more news and gossip, Melissa thanked her sister for the phone call and swore that she would be there the next day.

Abby was more than thrilled. She couldn't wait to see Melissa again.

Hours later, Abby got ready for bed feeling like a different person. Maybe things will work out after all, she concluded.

Abby smiled as she was falling asleep. It would be the first time since she found out that Casey had died, that she felt almost normal. She kissed the 8x10 picture of Casey, which was sitting on the bedside table, and turned out the light.

The next morning, Melissa got into her car and drove the two hours to be with her younger sister. She was grateful to be able to be close to Abby again. It had been too long since they were together.

Melissa was different from other people. She always had a 6th sense about her, which made her feel like she didn't fit in.

As a teenager, Melissa dabbled in wish craft. She found the world of magic and spells fascinating and it kept her attention up to this point. She mastered a few simple spells by the time she turned 14. By 17, she had had enough of school and was already working as a data entry clerk for the local newspaper.

She was happy by herself, learning new spells and improving her craft, but miserable around others.

At 24 years old, she met a man in the magic shop downtown. Melissa didn't marry him, but had a brief affair which produced a delightful baby girl. She named the child, Echo Prudence Hudson.

Echo, at 6 years old, was already showing signs of having extra sensory perception.

Echo got out of the car first and ran quickly towards Abby's home. Her shoulder-length, shiny, blond, very curly hair, bounced up and down as she bolted across the lawn.

"Echo!" her mother called, but the little girl was too excited to listen. Melissa watched as her free-spirited daughter raced ahead.

Abby heard the commotion outside and hurried to open the door.

Echo saw her aunt and squealed in delight as her little legs carried her faster than ever.

Abby gazed at her niece who was **running a mad dash**, her face all lit up inside. "You made it!" she shouted to the young child. She opened her arms and waited for the embrace.

Abby then looked up and saw her sister walking quickly towards the house. She let go of Echo's small frame and moved herself down the cement stairs where she waited with her arms wide open.

"Thanks for coming, sis", she whispered with pure joy into Melissa's ear as she wrapped her arms lovingly around her sister's body.

"The pleasure is all mine." Melissa loved the feeling of being in Abby's company again. It felt different, happier, and Melissa liked that the bad vibes were now gone.

They all hugged and then visited inside of Abby's home for a mere eight minutes before they started on their adventure.

CHAPTER FOUR

"Can we go now?" whined Echo who was anxious to start driving. She had heard many stories throughout the years about the old farmhouse from her grandma, and wanted to see if any of them were true.

Both sisters looked at each other and nodded. Neither Melissa nor Abby had seen the farmhouse since they were children. They both knew that this was going to be a rather exhilarating experience and they were all very excited to get started.

"Shall we take my car?" Abby offered as she put the key into the outside lock of her door. Melissa and Echo both agreed as it was the bigger of the two vehicles. They stopped for gas and a quick bite to eat and then they were on their way.

Twenty minutes later, the small group was on the highway which would lead them to the farmhouse.

The drive took about an hour in total. They talked, laughed, got caught up with each other's lives, sang along with the radio, and played games with the passing cars. As they got closer to their destination, they all studied the countryside and saw how each person's property got further and further apart from one another.

Then came the road which they needed to turn onto. Abby started the blinker to indicate a left-hand turn. She moved the steering wheel and soon they all saw the old farmhouse off in the distance. She drove up slowly to drink in every detail.

The farmhouse was indeed old and looked like it hadn't been lived in in years.

Abby was suddenly having second thoughts when she

finally parked the car. But with Echo's enthusiasm and Melissa's encouragement, she didn't have a chance to back away. Once the car door opened, the youngest of the three dashed towards the house to catch tiny pieces of the adventure ahead.

Melissa stood by the car and endearingly admired the old place and its immediate surroundings. "It hasn't really changed that much, eh?" Melissa turned to her sister and waited for an opinion.

Abby placed a flat hand against her brow to block out the sun and looked towards the farmhouse. "I'm not sure how much it's changed", she hesitated. "It's been too long since we've been on the property."

Melissa walked around the car and grabbed Abby's arm. "So let's see more", she said bravely. She was as excited as Echo to start this adventure. Together the sisters walked arm-in-arm up the long sidewalk towards the old house.

Abby turned this way and that, and studied everything she could as she walked; the sights, the smells, and the sounds.

Echo opened the front door and paused. As soon as she got inside, she could feel something out of the ordinary. The air seemed cold and musty and there were strange, eerie vibes all around her. She walked inside a tiny bit more and saw a man trying to hide behind a wall.

The frightened man had a faint white glow about him, and though his features were quite clear, Echo could almost see right through him.

Echo walked a bit closer and smiled at him but he didn't look in her direction. Seems he was more interested in what the two older girls were doing just outside of the door.

"Hello?" the little girl said softly so not to scare him. When he didn't pay any attention to her, Echo put her hands on her hips and cocked her head to one side. She could never understand why she could see these people and no-one else could. She knew they were not there to hurt her and has been proven right each and every time.

Echo turned her upper body and looked back at her aunt and mom who had just walked into the house. She watched and waited for their reaction to the man. When none came, Echo realized that neither of them had a problem with him being there, so she ran off to play.

The sisters came in after the young girl and Melissa too, could feel a strange presence almost immediately. Her ability with paranormal phenomenas was not as strong as Echo's, but she could definitely feel something odd inside the old home.

Melissa took a few more steps and got strong shivers up her spine once she got six feet inside the front door. The room was cold and daunting, and after looking around for a minute, she noticed that not a single window was open.

Melissa shook her hands from the wrists and blinked her eyes several times to try and brush the odd feelings away. No matter how hard she tried, Melissa could not shake the eerie sensations that were surrounding her being.

Besides the coldness in the air and the strange vibes all around her, she also felt as though there were a pair of angry eyes watching them, wanting them to leave and wondering why they were even there.

Melissa looked over at her sister, debating if she too could feel what she was feeling.

Abby was in awe as she was giving the old home the proverbial once-over. "What a wonder place", she sighed to herself as she took one small step after another around the front room.

Melissa smiled as she watched her sister's face light up. Once she sensed that Abby could not feel the oddness that she was feeling, Melissa decided to shrug it off until she got her sister's permission to dig deeper.

Abby walked through the small abode and touched and smelled everything. She liked the strange emptiness that it portrayed, the dust everywhere, and the loneliness that she felt as she walked from room to room. The house felt void, and yet it had character.

When she closed her eyes, Abby could feel the ambience of a houseful of people in the front room and she liked how welcoming it made her feel.

Echo was in a playful mood after having to sit still for so long in the back seat of Abby's car. With her arms out from her sides and her lips making a motor sound, Echo ran around the house pretending that she was an old fighter plane.

Melissa could hear her daughter's heavy footsteps dashing all over the place. "Echo!" her mother called. "Don't get into trouble!"

"I won't", she replied over her shoulder while continuing to play. Echo was running around, minding her own business, when she found the ghost man cowering behind yet another wall. She stood quietly and watched him for a minute before surprising him.

Brenner was observing the two sisters touching and moving everything in his home and he hated it. He didn't know why they were there but he wanted them to leave.

Echo had enough of watching him. She reached out and poked Brenner in the back. "You're it!" she teased and ran away.

Brenner was spooked by her forwardness and couldn't help but be amazed that the little girl could see him. Could the others, he wondered?

He turned back towards them and cautiously waved his hand in their direction. When they didn't react, he tried harder. When they still didn't respond, he walked over and placed himself in the middle of the room, then jumped up and down while waving both hands wildly, all over the place.

Echo felt the man's extreme energy and came back down the hall. She was stunned to find him in the same room as her mom and aunt. She saw what he was doing and it made her laugh. "You're being silly!" Echo kidded as she came closer and looked straight into Brenner's eyes.

Brenner was more than surprised. He couldn't breathe and suppressed any more movement.

Abby turned around and saw Echo in the middle of the room. Thinking that her niece was speaking to her she asked, "What are you talking about?"

Echo pointed to the man who was not jumping around anymore, but instead was becoming terrified at having been found out. "He's silly!" she shouted with laughter in her voice.

Brenner froze in his tracks. His 'please-don't-tell-on-me' expression was pitiful and he wasn't sure what he should do next. Brenner closed his eyes real tight and held his breath. When nothing happened, he turned and looked at Echo's smiling face.

Abby looked towards her sister. "What's she talking about?"

Without moving anything but his head, Brenner turned and looked at both women to see how they were reacting to the situation.

Melissa looked around the quaint room and spied a large stuffed rabbit with long floppy ears lying on the nearby armchair. She walked towards it and picked it up. The small hairs were standing straight up in the back of her neck as Melissa walked past the middle of the room.

"Yes, he is silly, isn't he darling?" Melissa agreed. As she walked back to her daughter and handed Echo the stuffed toy, Melissa felt a cold presence as she glided across the floor again. "I'll bet it would be okay if I gave this to you", she said trying to ignore the odd sensations.

Brenner held his breath and kept his statuette pose as Melissa brushed by him a second time. This time she was within inches of where he stood.

Echo wasn't sure why her mother had made that gesture, but she happily took the toy from her loving arms. Then she turned around, waved bye to Brenner, and ran around the house again. Seconds later, she had completely forgotten about the three grown-ups that she had left standing in the front room.

Brenner remained in his same stance. He was terrified to move for fear of being found out.

Melissa reached Abby's side and then turned around slowly as her eyes scanned the entire room again. She felt an odd coldness somewhere close by her, but she couldn't pinpoint where.

Melissa looked into her sister's happy face and wondered if she should confide in her; tell her what she was thinking.

Abby was glowing inside. She loved how she felt inside these four walls. It had a nice homey feeling.

After seeing Abby's content expression, Melissa decided to keep this information to herself, at least for now. She could definitely feel someone else in the small area with them, but she didn't want to scare Abby. Then she remembered Echo's words. She knew that there had to be something more to Echo's rantings. The little girl was not prone to just say things that were not true.

Melissa needed to check things out a bit more before she would come forward with any information.

Oblivious to what was going on around her, Abby was smiling and enjoying the sights and sounds inside the old farmhouse. She moved towards the feature wall and stood in front of the large pane of glass. She looked out the window, across the lawn, and saw the old weeping willow tree. How magnificent, she declared in her mind. The tree had grown so much since the last time she'd seen it.

Abby looked straight down and saw the old wooden

boards that were held together to make the large porch. She wondered how old it was now.

Abby turned around as if she were a ballerina, and looked at the room that they were standing in; the walls, the furniture, and the floor. She closed her eyes, as if in a happy trance, and felt the ambiance in the cozy room. She spread her arms out to the open air and could almost feel herself being transported back to the past where the room was filled with people laughing and enjoying themselves in this very spot.

Abby stopped her mild dancing for a quick second. Her face lit up with a large smile and it wasn't long before she had made up her mind to escape the real world and move here. She turned to her sister and niece and asked them for their advice. "So, what do you guys think?"

Despite their reservations, everyone agreed that it was for the best.

Melissa secretly had a doubt, but never let on. She hummed and hawed about whether Abby should move here or stay where she was, but she also knew that her sister needed a change of scenery. Although she couldn't help but shake the thought that something wasn't right inside the old farmhouse, Melissa knew that Abby needed a different place to live; a place where her heart could mend.

Melissa figured that the feelings that she was experiencing, why she felt so odd inside the old farmhouse, would reveal themselves soon enough. For now, she would let Abby have her moment.

"I guess this will be my new home then, eh?" Abby commented happily to the air.

Brenner bent his body around quickly to get a better look in Abby's direction. What did she mean *her* home? This is my home, he muttered under his breath.

Brenner became furious and couldn't bear to hear anymore. Realizing now that the women couldn't see him, he moved from his vogue position and walked away pouting. He didn't know when they had planned to move in, but he would make sure that it wouldn't be for long.

When they had nothing else to look at, the sisters decided it was time to leave. Abby ushered Melissa and Echo out the door so she could have one more look around the place in private.

Abby walked around quickly, smiling proudly at becoming the new owner of the farmhouse. "Hello, my new home", she whispered to the openness of the room. "I'll be back soon." She stood in the front entrance with the key in her hand as she sighed.

With the door now tightly closed and locked, Abby ran to be with her small family. The sisters locked arms and walked together to the car while Echo ran ahead.

Abby pressed her free hand on top of her other hand that was already linked under Melissa's elbow. "I'm going to be happy here, right?" She looked into her sister's face and waited for her to reply.

Melissa smiled and nodded in Abby's direction. She didn't know what to say so she kept quiet. She had such a strange feeling about the place but didn't know what to make of it.

"I think so too." Abby released her hold on her sister's arm and helped Echo into the back seat. After she fastened the little girl's seat belt, she went to the driver's side of the car and sat down.

Melissa opened the heavy metal door and turned around to look at the old farmhouse one more time before getting into the car. Her eyes couldn't help but scale up the side of the house towards the roof.

Melissa gasped and her neck involuntarily moved forward as her eyes widened in shock. She could swear that there was someone standing in the upstairs window looking down at them.

"All set?" Abby cheered as she put her mid-sized car into gear.

Melissa wanted to say something to Abby, but changed her mind when the car was put into drive. Melissa diverted her eyes for a second, sat down in her seat, and closed her door. She then turned and looked again at the upstairs window. This time there was nobody there.

Maybe it was my imagination, she thought sadly, but she couldn't tear her eyes away. As the car rolled forward, she switched the sight of her eyes to the front window of the car and decided to keep this information to herself. At least for the moment.

Echo sat in the back seat and leaned forward to see what her mother was looking at. With her tiny face pushed gently against the clear glass, a smile blossomed on her lips when she saw him. Echo waved good-bye to her friend who was now in the upstairs window. She was pleased that he had come to say good-bye.

Brenner had a hard time believing that the little girl could see him while the others could not. He didn't know what to make of this, but as long as they were driving away, he didn't care.

Her friend didn't wave back, which didn't concern her. Echo knew that these ghost people get all confused because she could see them and touch them. Not everyone had that ability.

She also wasn't concerned that neither her mom nor her aunt made mention of the strange man. She knew that sometimes grown-ups couldn't see the same things that she could see, and she has learned to adjust to that fact.

Once they were a few feet away from the property, Echo reclined in her padded chair, put the headphones on top of her head, and listened to the music that streamed from her ipod.

The sisters talked the whole way back about Abby moving and where to put the furniture. Now that Abby had a look inside again, she could see where things from her old place would go in the new one. It made her sad to think that some of her items would be left behind.

They arrived back at Abby's home within the hour and then said their good-byes. Both girls had work in the morning and Echo had school. Melissa smiled and promised that she would now visit and call more often.

"I would love that!" shouted Abby as she silently wished for them to stay longer.

While Melissa drove home with her daughter, her mind was on the vision that she saw in the upstairs window. Was it her imagination, or was it real? Why could she see him in the window and not in the same room?

Melissa turned to her daughter and wanted to ask her if

she saw anything odd while they were in the farmhouse, but then stopped herself. She knew that seeing things and people were not out of the ordinary for Echo. Instead, Melissa decided to ask the question flat out.

"Echo?" Melissa reflected in a question state, but got no response. She turned around to find out why her daughter didn't answer and noticed that Echo had had enough of the day and was now out for the count. "Never mind", Melissa chuckled. "I'll ask you later."

CHAPTER FIVE

The following day was Monday. Abby got up in a happy mood after dreaming all night about the farmhouse. She was pleased with her decision of moving and couldn't wait to tell her boss her thoughts.

By the beginning of the first coffee break, Abby felt the timing was right. She knew exactly where her boss would be and what he would be doing. With her shoulders back and hours of debating under her belt, Abby marched to her boss's office to give him her notice.

Knock, knock!

Mr. Alex Quan was startled by the gentle knock at his closed door. He looked up and was immediately pleased to see Abby standing at the square window, waiting for entrance to his office.

"Abby!" he called as he stood up and walked across the carpeted room.

Abby was already pushing the heavy wooden door open and coming inside. She hoped that he wouldn't mind her forwardness.

"Can I have a moment of your time, sir?" she asked nervously as she poked in through the slightly opened door.

Mr. Quan smiled as he extended his hand in her direction. "Of course, come in!" He immediately offered her his condolences as he held her hand inside both of his.

Mr. Quan was saddened by the news of her fiancé passing away, and had already sent the mandatory bouquet of flowers to her home, but this was the first time that he'd seen her since the day before she got the news. He was delighted when she phoned last week to say that she was finally ready to come back to work.

Abby was happy to be in his presence. "Nice to see you again, Mr. Quan", she said.

"Please, sit down", he offered as his hand made a sweeping motion to the chair in front of his desk. He put both hands on the back of the chair that sat opposite his desk. He waited for her to be completely seated and then he went around to his own chair.

"Thank you", she replied with sadness in her voice. 'You're very kind." Abby wasn't comfortable in this room. It always felt like she was in the principle's office, but today she needed to be here to say what she came for.

Mr. Quan could see that she was anxious, but he didn't know why.

"First, I want to say thank you for letting me have so much time off", Abby began, forcing happiness into her voice.

Mr. Quan watched with interest as he could see there was more to come. He folded his hands on top of the desk and begged her to continue. "Abby? What is it?"

Abby's tears gently and slowly escaped from their confines and rolled gracefully down her cheeks as she explained the plan to her boss. While the words were tumbling out of her mouth, they all of a sudden didn't make as much sense to her as Abby had first thought.

Yesterday she believed that living in the farmhouse would be a great idea. Now, saying the words out loud, she had a doubt.

Mr. Quan felt a great deal of empathy towards his

favorite employee. She was not only the same age as his daughter, Petra, who died almost fourteen years ago in a swimming class at school, but she had the same features and demeanor.

It was so uncanny for Mr. Quan to lose a daughter and then interview her look-a-like for a position with his company. Yes, her resume fit the job which was advertised, but the odds of her getting hired tripled when he realized all the commonalities of the two girls.

Working with Abby over the past few years, was like watching his own daughter go through life. Mr. Quan thought about what Abby had just experienced, and what would be best for her right now. He then decided that she really needed to take a bit more time for herself.

"I agree", he said supporting her decision whole-heartedly. Mr. Quan knew the opportunity with the farmhouse was too good to pass up. While he didn't want to lose her as an employee, or from his life, he decided to extend her leave of absence. That way, if in a few months from now she wanted to come back, she could.

He saw her tears and handed her the box of Kleenex which sat on the edge of his desk. He offered her to take as many tissues as she wished.

"Peyton took over your paperwork while you've been gone and he has been doing a very fine job", he began. "I'm sure that he will be quite pleased to continue doing it for another little while."

Abby was gratefully relieved. "Thank you for understanding", she sobbed. She came around to his side of the desk and gave her employer a big hug.

Mr. Quan saw her stand up and he immediately got up from his black leather chair. They embraced and it made him feel like a dad again. He only wanted the best for Abby and he hoped that this would put her one step closer to her dream.

"So, how about you start right away?" he declared to a surprised Abby.

Abby smiled and nodded, hoping that it would really be okay.

"Done deal!" he shouted. They said their good-byes and he wished her well, with promises that she'd keep in touch.

Abby walked down the long hallway and cleaned out her desk and surrounding area. She said good-bye to her favorite people and off she went.

Abby sat in her car and cried. She felt relieved, but dismayed. What will I do if I don't work, she wondered.

Abby pushed that thought aside and tried to focus on what to do next. She pulled her small note pad out of her purse and crossed out the first line. "Done", she said quietly to herself. The next line read: talk to landlord. As Abby pulled out into traffic, she felt a bit better about her decision to move.

Abby's next stop was at her landlord's office. She called him on her cell phone to say that she was on her way over to see him. "Hi Mr. Humphries. It's Abby Hudson calling."

While he had no problem taking a meeting with her, he wanted to know what it was all about.

"I'm moving and I'd like to give my notice", she stated rather formally.

Mr. Humphries was not happy about losing Abby as a tenant. She was always on time for her rent, never made any noise, or had given him any problems. "I'm very sorry that you're leaving", he said sincerely. "May I ask why?"

Abby kept her attention on the road ahead of her while she explained the situation with the farmhouse to her landlord. She also told Mr. Humphries that she had just taken another leave of absence from work as she really felt that she needed more time away from the world as she knew it.

The man on the other end of the line went quiet for a few seconds. "I see", he finally uttered. "Well, what can I say but I will miss you."

"Thank you", was all she could muster. Abby suddenly realized that she was tearing all ties to her old life and moving into the unknown. Her body was beginning to go into a panic mode and she needed to calm down. "Do I need to sign any paperwork, or do I just give you my notice over the phone?"

"Now that I know that you're thinking of moving, I can do the rest on my end", he offered trying to make things easier for her. "No need for you to come here at all." He could hear that her voice was trembling and he became concerned.

Mr. Humphries knew that the man that Abby was living with in the small rented home, had not been around much lately. He put two-and-two together and came up with the fact that they had split up and he had already moved out.

Mr. Humphries knew enough not to pry. "When will you be out?" he asked delicately.

Abby had all the time in the world as she had no dead-lines or restrictions. She wasn't sure if it would take her two weeks or three weeks to get everything out so she didn't have a firm answer to give him. "Can I say the middle of the month?"

Mr. Humphries looked at the nearby calendar. His index finger went up to the small box that surrounded today's date and saw that the middle would be in nineteen days. "That will put us to January 15. I think that will be just fine."

"Thank you for understanding."

They said their good-byes and Abby was told to drive straight home. She made a couple of stops along the way but arrived two hours later.

Posted on the outside of her door was a white envelope. Abby ripped it open and inside was a short letter from her landlord. It read:

My Dear Miss Abigail Hudson;

I am going to miss you as a tenant, and as a person. I have finished the mere paperwork that was needed and now you are free to go. Please note that I have enclosed a cheque for your damage deposit, as well as the interest that has uncured since you gave me the money. I have every ounce of confidence that the place will be perfect when you leave and I pray the extra cash will help you with your new adventure.

I hope the wind stays on your back and the sun is

always on your bright face. I wish you much luck and happiness for your future.

Should you ever find yourself without a home, you can always contact me.

Mr. Humphries signed a lovely greeting and put his signature on the bottom of the letter. He also added a smiling happy face in blue pen underneath.

Abby stared down at the beautifully hand-written note and cried. It was touching and a very nice gesture. She made a mental note to thank him for this at a later date. For now, she put the things from the office away and went into the kitchen to make herself something to eat. She knew that the next few days were going to be full of things to do, and hard on her mind and body.

Abby decided that she didn't want to face anything more for the rest of today. She was assured that the other three items on her 'things-to-do-list' could wait until tomorrow.

*   *   *   *

Pulling up in front of Abby's home was scary. He wasn't sure how he would be accepted, let alone be invited inside. The tall man put the car into park and checked his appearance in the rearview mirror. "Good enough", he muttered. He stepped out of the car and walked up to her front door. "Here goes", he breathed for luck.

Ding Dong!

Abby stopped what she was doing and went to answer the door. Surprise is not the word Abby first thought of when she saw Officer Nick Gatling's face grinning back at her. She couldn't open the door fast enough. "Officer Gatling!" she called with a great deal of enthusiasm.

"Evening", he said shyly. "Just in the neighbourhood and thought I'd check to see how you were doing." He stuck his hands into the front pockets of his pants, hiked his shoulders up around his ears, and was beginning to kick the toes of his shoes against the cement ground.

Abby was thrilled to see him. "Please, come on in." Abby pulled the sleeve on one of his arms and almost dragged him inside.

"Have a seat." She motioned towards the couch by the wall after he took his shoes off. Abby followed behind him but took a seat on the smaller couch.

"So, you just came to see how I was doing?" She cocked her head to one side and looked like a little girl. She didn't remember him to be this handsome. Abby was nervous and started playing with her hands in her lap.

Officer Gatling was beaming with pride that, not only was she pleased to see him, she let him inside of her home. "I did, and please call me Nick." He used both hands to move his jean jacket apart so she could see that he was not wearing a uniform or hiding a gun. "I'm a civilian today", he joked. "I'm off-duty."

"Nick." She said the name out loud to see how it would sound. "Yes, I could say that."

He let out a small puff of air, more for nerves than anything else. "So, tell me, how have you been?" He really wanted to know. He wanted to come by so many times but the cop-side of his personality talked him out of it. Today, though, he decided to come no matter what.

"I think I'm fine", she said slowly. "Or at least I will be." Abby thought about the reasons behind her answer and then rolled her eyes before she started speaking again. "I have made some decisions that will allow me to be fine in the long run."

"Oh?" Nick was intrigued. This woman was so much happier than the last time he had seen her. He could really get a glimpse of who the real Abby was this time, and he liked her. Nick sat back and waited to hear what she had to say.

Abby suddenly remembered her dinner and all the fixings that were still lying around exposed on the kitchen counter. "Have you eaten yet?" she asked trying to buy more time with him.

Nick was both shocked by the question, but pleased with the offer. He wasn't sure that he should bother her for food, though.

Before he could utter another word, Abby spoke up. "I was just making myself some supper and I wouldn't mind the company." She stood up and gently forced him into the kitchen.

Nick reluctantly stood up and followed right behind her. He removed his jean jacket as he walked and draped it handsomely on the back of the kitchen chair. "Need any help?" he asked as he looked around to see what she was making.

Abby took stock of the items that she was about to prepare and saw that she did indeed have enough for two. She turned to him and responded. "I was about to have a simple meal of fish sticks with Kraft dinner. Still interested?" she asked while making a face and keeping one eye closed tightly.

Nick saw the look and laughed. "Mmm. Sounds good."

Abby threw the nearby tea towel in his direction. "Whatever." Secretly, she wished that she was serving something more elegant, but who knew that she would be having a guest?

During the preparation, they talked about his job and what he likes and doesn't like about it. While they were eating, Abby told Nick about moving and taking another leave of absence.

Soon the meal was done and they realized that they had talked for more than two hours. They placed their dishes in the sink and Nick insisted on helping with the cleaning up.

"Don't you dare try to clean in my house!" she ordered playfully over her shoulder. "I'll do the rest in a while, or maybe I'll wait until tomorrow morning."

Nick looked at the time and guessed that maybe he had stayed long enough. "It was really nice connecting again. I'm glad you are, and will be okay."

"Oh, you're leaving?"

"I probably should, early work day tomorrow."

Abby was crushed but hoped for another visit soon. "Okay. Thanks for coming by, Nick", she gushed. "It was nice to see you again."

She asked him to wait for a second and then handed him a small piece of paper. "Here's the new address, should you ever find your way to my *new* neck of the woods", she laughed.

Nick studied the information and then stuck it into the little pocket on the front of his shirt. "I might just do that."

"Good." She was pleased with the thought that he'd come by another time. "Take care and thanks again for your company." She touched his arm in an intimate manner as he stepped over the stoop.

"Bye, Abby." Nick was pleased with himself for making the effort to see this beautiful woman. He'd never gotten her out of his heart or mind, and knew that she needed time to herself. He was so relived that she looked so much better than the last visit, and he hoped that maybe, in a month or two, that she'd like to go out with him sometime.

Nick patted his pocket that held her new address. "I'll see you soon."

Abby closed the door and walked to the living room window. She watched Nick get into a small blue car and then drive away. "Huh", she whispered. "Imagine that."

*　　*　　*　　*

Almost 10:30pm and Abby had lots to say but nobody to say them to. She called her mom to let her know the details of her day, and started with Officer Nick.

Elizabeth was surprised when she was told that one of the officers had come by to check in on Abby. She'd never heard of this before but she was pleased with the practice. "Is he a nice man?" she inquired as a mother making sure that her daughter was in good hands.

"I think so." Abby's mind drifted back to the short amount of time that Nick was in her home.

Abby continued and told her mother about the rest of her morning and afternoon.

Elizabeth could hear the tone in her daughter's voice as she spoke and it made her sad. She heard about how Abby felt going in to see her boss, and then speaking with her landlord on the drive home. She heard Abby almost fall apart as she stated that there's nothing left to do but pack and move.

Elizabeth wasn't sure what she should do. "Do you want me to come over?" She stopped breathing so she could hear the answer.

Abby took a second before she replied. She looked around the very familiar room and then decided that she didn't want to do anything but go to bed for tonight. "I'll be okay, mom, but thanks."

Elizabeth listened as only a mother could, to her daughter's words and tone. She tried to find the space that begged her to come over, but didn't find one so she backed off. "Okay, Abby. But if you need me, you know I'm only a phone call away."

"Yes, mom." Abby rolled her eyes and giggled at the thought that her mom always wanted to take care of her. Abby was a grown woman with her own place and her own job. She leased a car, paid her own bills, and bought her own food, but her mother still worried about her. While it was frustrating at times, it was also very nice to be loved so much.

"Good night darling."

"Good night, mom."

CHAPTER SIX

Chapter Six

Abby had a little cry before falling asleep, but woke up feeling more energized. She now couldn't wait to get started on her new life. After eating her breakfast and drinking her coffee, she stood up and began her mission.

Abby was nervous as she took the suitcases out of the closet and moved boxes from room to room. She knew what she was doing was right, but in the back of her mind she was still harboring on whether moving was a good thing or not.

All day she kept flipping back and forth, trying to decide if she should stay or go. Several times Abby had to force herself to open drawers and take things off of hangers because she knew otherwise, she would never have the courage.

Abby hated moving Casey's things. She also hated the thought that he would never wear 'this' or 'that' again. Forty minutes later, she was sitting on the floor in the spare room and sifting through his baseball card collection, his small collection of trophies from high school, and his large collection of cologne. Abby then got to the clothing.

She lifted up one of his shirts and tried to guess which two fragrances he used that day. She laughed when she could only recognize one.

Abby pushed the shirt into her face and cried as she remembered asking him near the beginning of their relationship, why he was putting on two different colognes.

Casey laughed and said that he wanted to be unique. "Anyone can wear one scent, darlin', but I wanna keep 'em guessing", he replied with a cheesy grin as tried to grab her.

"But I only wear one scent at a time", she giggled and turned slightly to get out of his reach.

Casey started following behind her. "But you already smell like a treat, darling. Now, come here so I can eat you up!" he playfully ordered.

He ran after her until he caught her, then he nibbled on her neck and shoulders until their lips found each other.

Abby dried her eyes and placed the newly folded shirt into the box. She gave it a final loving smooth-down and kept going. She put as much as she could of his things into each box, and then labeled them and put them aside. Since Casey had no family, Abby would give the clothes, shoes, and other usable items to the homeless shelter downtown.

Of course, there were a few items of Casey's that Abby wanted to keep for the rest of her life. She put those treasures inside of a few different boxes as if she were stealing them from a living soul.

When the master and second bedroom were all packed up, Abby walked around her home and touched the other special treasures, reveling in their memories. She shed a few more tears and then she knew that she should move on.

With a framed 8x10 picture of Casey clutched close to her chest, she had to sit on the couch for a second. Once she calmed down a bit, she remembered that she had not made arrangements for a truck yet. It was getting close to the end of December and she hoped that she would have no problems booking the large vehicle.

Abby got the phone book out and found the number of

a moving company that her mom had suggested. She immediately called the movers and set a time and date for them to come. "Ten o'clock will be fine", she muttered sadly under her breath. She hung up and looked around, suddenly realizing that there was still a lot left to do. She sighed and took another few minutes to herself before she got up and started packing again.

Melissa called around mid-afternoon and offered to help. Abby thanked her but refused insisting that she wanted to do it herself.

Abby wanted to touch and say good-bye to each item that would not be going with her to the new place. She wanted to sort through everything herself and hoped that her sister would understand.

Melissa dissolved into tears for her little sister. She tried to understand how hard this must be for Abby, and then reluctantly allowed her to continue the work herself. "Call me when you're ready."

"I love you."

"I love you too."

At 1pm, sixteen days later, the last piece of furniture was moved onto the truck. Abby's feet were firmly in place as she looked at the outside of her former home. She stood there for a few minutes before she finally turned to face the movers. "I need a minute", she said sadly. She watched them nod knowingly and then she walked back inside and had another quick look around.

It looked and felt so very different. It held no life or inklings of people having been in there. What used to be her happy home was now an empty shell. It still held her thoughts, her tears, her laughter, her heartaches, and her private moments, but the silence was so unbearable. Her home was now echoing from the pain of her leaving.

Without warning, the emotional part of Abby got the better of her. She suddenly collapsed and fell to her knees. As the tears streamed from both eyes, she grabbed the shagged carpet with her fingers and cried out of despair for her former life. "I don't want to go, Casey", she whimpered. "Why did you have to leave me?"

Abby's face fell down onto her folded arms. She was now laying flat upon the bluish-grey carpet and wanted to die. What used to be her happy home was now cold and very lonely. Without Casey, it wasn't a home anymore. "How do I go on without you?"

Abby needed a few more minutes before she could sit up and compose herself. She knew that she had to go, and now would be as good as time as any.

Abby took one more look around her tiny home, inspecting the ceiling, floors, and windows. "Good-bye home-sweet-home!" she called as she grabbed the inside door knob for the last time.

As Abby closed the door to her old life, she knew that she was walking away from her past, but going towards an unknown future.

Abby put the key in the lock and froze. Shutting the door for the last time was rough. This was a home that she had shared with Casey for 2 years. Never once did she think it would end. She had hoped that when Casey came back from this most recent business trip that they might finally get married and move forward with their life. Casey's death put an end to that dream.

Abby pulled the key out and sadly walked towards her car while nodding to the driver of the moving van that she was now ready to go. She watched as he nodded back and put the large truck into gear. Soon the two vehicles were both off and on their way to her new life.

Seventy-two minutes later, as Abby drove up the long dirt driveway that led to the courtyard of her new home, she tried to envision the next chapter of her life.

Abby saw that the movers had already arrived and were now waiting for her to unlock the front door. She parked her car just outside of the worn-out picket fence and said her hellos to the men as she emerged from her car. She smiled shyly towards them but the sentiment was not returned.

The movers were not happy, merely relieved that she had finally arrived.

Once Abby unlocked the front door, she stood back to allow the four movers to do their work.

Abby walked back to the edge of the sidewalk that led to the front entrance of her yard and turned around to take in the view. The slight breeze that grazed her body and hair, smelled of old pastures and farm animals, but she didn't mind.

As she turned slowly and scanned the vast country-side, she saw how much distance there was between her new home and her neighbor's. She placed a stiff hand up against her eyebrows to block out the sun from her eyes and viewed all that she could. She could see miles and miles around her without another person in sight.

She then turned to look at the entrance of her new home.

It was exactly 35 feet from the small, white, worn-out gate to the Victorian-style porch, which needed painting badly. Not one of the first projects, but it was certainly on her list of 'things-to-do'.

Abby took a long quiet moment as she gingerly leaned against her 2007 Grand Marquis and watched the movers do their work. She studied everything that she could, all around the place that she would call home; at least for the next little while.

She marveled at the historic architecture of the old building - its windows and porch. How the angles suited the place, how the shutters and doorframe matched, and how it almost felt like home already. It was breathtaking and it was all hers.

Abby's head whipped around when she heard a small commotion coming from the back of the truck. She then noticed that her very expensive cello was being lifted out of the large heavy vehicle and she hustled to give it her personal guidance.

"I'll take that", she yelled as she intercepted the cello from the second mover's clumsy hands.

Abby grabbed it and held the instrument delicately in her arms as she looked her precious item over to make sure that it was still in perfect order. Completely satisfied that its journey was made safely, she sighed with great relief and brought the cello into her new home.

As the large furniture got taken off the truck and went past her into the house, she scampered around, instructing the men where to put her valuable things.

Brenner was sitting on the window seat near the back of

his home and could hear strange sounds in the rooms below him. He had been alone for so long and he didn't expect nor want company. He grumbled that it must be an animal that found its way inside and tried to ignore it but the sounds not only continued, they became louder.

After a while, the noise of shuffling, scraping, dragging, and soft humming consumed him to the point where he needed to check it out.

Brenner walked slowly, trying to pinpoint where the sounds were coming from. He found the room, placed both hands against the door frame and peaked around the corner trying not to expose too much of himself.

Brenner was surprised to see a very beautiful girl moving things around in his mother's favorite area. He was shocked at first and wanted to scream out, but instead he just waited. He watched this stranger as she stood back and admired her work, but who was she, he wondered. And why was she touching things that did not belong to her?

Brenner then remembered her face from a few weeks ago. She was here with the little girl who could see him. This intrigued him even more. But why was she here all alone, he wondered.

He watched her for another little while before retreating back to his room. Once he confirmed that she wasn't stealing things, but merely moving things around, he felt a bit better. But why, he wondered as he headed off to the upstairs bedroom. Why was she in his home again?

Hours later, with the truck and men gone and everything now in its proper place, Abby was able to sit on the couch and enjoy her new environment. She liked what she saw and how it felt to be free of the city and her old life, however, it felt odd to be inside this new place that held no history or memories for her. It felt empty and old. It had a feeling of life, but not hers.

As Abby scanned the room, seeing some of her things mixed with a few of the previous owner's things, she felt out of place. She knew a pep-talk was in order. She sat up and straightened her shoulders. "It's going to be your new home, and in a day or two, it will even start to feel like that", she gushed to herself while looking around the newly-set up room. She was trying to convince herself that she would be okay in this new environment. That it will just take time. She smiled with the thought that soon she will have memories of being in here, experiences that she will be able to look back on and smile.

This was a new start, a new beginning. She had a strong feeling that she would find her smile in this new place. She had lost it a few weeks ago with the sad news that her fiancé, Casey, had died in a plane crash. The tears hidden behind her eyes willed her to cry as she thought back to that terrible moment.

"No!" Abby shouted as her body stiffened again. "I'm not going to cry!" She stood up as if to brush away the sad memories. She walked quickly to the room that was now designated as her music room and looked for her music sheets.

She sat down on the light-colored wooden chair with the round, spindly back, sitting in the middle of the room, and placed the large dark cello between her legs. She found the song that she wanted to play and placed the sheet music front and centre on the black metal stand.

She then leaned over and hit the switch on her cassette player to bring more background music into the room. As the piano and violin music started their intro to the song, Abby sat up straight and prepared herself to play.

'A Whole New World' brought life into the once empty space while Abby waited for her cue to start playing. She held the large bow in her right hand and the neck of the cello in her left. On the down beat she moved her instrument into position and began to play.

Brenner heard the rich symphony of notes and slowly made his way back towards the room that used to belong to his mother. He peaked around the corner of the door frame, just as before, and watched as Abby's fingers lovingly stroked out the wonderful melody.

Abby closed her eyes and felt every vibe, every note, and tried to sing the words in her head as she played. Before the song had ended, she felt salty tears stream down the edges of her face and creep along the curvature of her neck.

A few bars later, she started to play harder as the words to the song played havoc in her mind. This is her new world now. Here, in this old house. Her life as she knew it was now done and it crushed her. The reality of it ripped through her emotional self and Abby found that her fingers were missing notes.

Abby abruptly stopped playing and turned the background music off with a smash of her hand. She let her emotions take hold of her as she released all of her frustration and anger at losing Casey. "I didn't want this", she cried. "I want things to be the way they were before."

Abby lashed out and the black metal stand went flying

across the room. She got up and ran, wiping away the water from her neck and face.

Brenner watched her in amazement as she flew past him in heated anger. She was not the enemy and now he knew it. He surmised that she was put here as roughly as he was.

Brenner made a hasty decision a long time ago and that's why he was there. It didn't look like this girl had a choice either, but at least she could leave if she wanted to. Unlike himself who's been locked away in the farmhouse for many decades.

Abby threw herself onto the bed that she had once shared with Casey, and sobbed for the next hour. The last few weeks had been torture for her and she didn't know why. She wanted it to stop, but she wasn't sure how it could Casey was gone. She was now living here. What else could change for her, she wondered.

Brenner followed closely behind her. He saw her tear-stained face and wanted so badly to reach out to her. In his ghostly state, he knew there was nothing he could do to comfort her. He took one last look in Abby's direction and then decided to leave her be with her thoughts and emotions.

An hour later, Abby resolved that it was time to get herself ready for bed. She washed her face and went to the bathroom, then walked around her home turning off the lights. Eventually she made it to the kitchen.

She reached into the fridge and poured herself a glass of chocolate milk. She drank it down in three gulps and walked back to her bedroom where she flopped herself on the bed in total exhaustion.

As Abby lay on her back, staring up at the ceiling, she thought about the last few weeks. "Crazy", she confirmed. "What could possibly top this?"

She rolled over onto her side, grabbed the blankets up to her neck, and closed her eyes. All she wanted to do now was sleep.

CHAPTER SEVEN

By the end of the next day, Abby was pretty much settled into her new home. "Only a few more things to unpack", she stated to the air. As she emptied her boxes, she placed her stuff beside a few of the old things that were already lying around on doilies on top of tables. She stood back and liked what she saw.

Brenner loved how she moved and looked. She was interesting and very beautiful to look at. He hadn't seen another soul in almost a decade and it pleased him to watch her in his home. He wasn't even minding her putting her things in with his mother's on the tables and other places.

Abby was hanging pictures and checking things out when she came upon a pull-down door in the ceiling, in the small hallway between the two bedrooms. Now things made sense.

Abby had found a make-shift ladder with extra large steps in the second bedroom, which was now her music room. The bulky, obviously home-made ladder was propped up in one corner of the large room. Abby moved it into the closet so it wouldn't be in the way. She didn't know what it was for, but was now pleased to have solved the puzzle.

Abby ran to get the odd ladder and placed it under the trap door. She climbed to the top rung and pulled on the large knob. The trap door opened easily and Abby's eyes widened in delight.

To Abby's surprise, there was another large room in the house. A room that looked like it had once been a boy's bedroom.

The room had been closed up after Brenner's death and the farm house had been sold years later. Brenner doesn't remember when, but it seems that he woke up one day and there were different people in the house. He wasn't sure why, or where his parents had gone, and so he stayed in his room ever since.

The new owners, two adults most of the time but children and other family came by often, never came upstairs. They lived in the home for almost twenty years and then moved to the city. Secretly, and with sadness in his heart, Brenner believed that he had chased them away. He remembers making a great deal of noise, but mostly at night, and tried to scare them all away. He believed them to be burglars and didn't want them in the house.

Once they were gone, he was alone again and then he missed their company. He promised himself that would not scare this young lady away.

Abby climbed higher and then stepped inside the large, very musty room. Instantly, the aura changed but she wasn't sure why. The air was thicker and the room held a strange coldness. She moved about slowly, trying not to touch anything but looking at absolutely everything.

The room was semi-dark, only one window shone light. She tried to find a light switch but none were found. She walked over to the boarded-up window and tried to pry the square piece of plywood off the opening with her bare hands. That didn't work.

Abby looked around for something else to help get the board off. She couldn't find anything in the upstairs bedroom, so she went downstairs where she remembered she had found a pair of knitting needles earlier in the day.

"Right where I thought you'd be", she expressed with

happiness. She ran back up the very strong staircase and began again.

It took a bit of work and at one point she hoped that she wouldn't break the painted metal stick. Once the last nail from the crude board was removed, the light came in and the room took on a new glow. After she realized what she had just done, Abby felt a very satisfied smile blossom across her face for the first time in months.

She turned around and inspected the room again. It felt peaceful and full of love. She adored the ambience that the room employed.

Abby loved the smell in the large, empty room above the kitchen. It was musty, dusty, and very cluttered but it felt nice to be in there. She knew that it would take a while to clean it up but knew it would be worth it. All of a sudden, she felt like she was home.

Brenner watched as Abby moved his favorite chair to the other side of the room. He wasn't sure if this bothered him or not, but he stood his ground and kept watching her. He was fascinated that she was even there.

Abby stood up and clapped her hands together and then wiped them down the front of her pants. "I'll get more started on this room tomorrow", she winced with disgust over the amount of dust on the furniture.

Brenner then saw her climb down the stairs and decided to follow carefully behind her. He was intrigued with what she had planned to do with his bedroom.

Brenner watched her straighten things up in the living room and kitchen while she continued touching everything in her midst.

Two hours later, as Abby yawned and stretched, she felt another day had come to an end. She turned the TV off and put herself to bed.

Brenner had stayed close by her side all day. He loved how she was now looking happier than when she first got there. Her minutes of crying were fewer and her humming to herself became constant. She certainly seemed like a nice person, he thought.

Once Abby was fast asleep, Brenner went to his room. He smiled as he realized that it felt good to have someone in the house with him again.

The next morning, right after breakfast, Abby went back upstairs. This time she felt an odd coldness all around her once she put both feet inside the room. She was not sure what it could be or where it was coming from, but thought that maybe there was a draft in the room. Her time was now used up finding the spot where the cold air was seeping through the cracks in the walls and windows.

Abby got down on her hands and knees and placed a flat hand against the entire length of baseboard on one wall. "Nothing."

Abby went against the next wall, and then the next. "Still nothing", she muttered. She moved towards the window and did the same thing against all four edges of the glass. "Mmph!" Abby crosses her arms in front of her chest and wondered where the cold air was coming from.

She started moving things around and then got frustrated to the point where she decided to worry about the coldness later.

Once the room looked appealing to her, Abby decided

that she'd done enough work for one day. "Tomorrow I will come back and dust and clean you", she playfully offered to the items in the room. She turned and waved to the room as if it was her friend. "Bye for now." She was cheery and made her way downstairs for something to eat.

Brenner kept a close eye on her but stayed back so as not to scare her. He liked having her around. She kept him from moping and thinking about his past and all of his mistakes. As long as things were going to be like this, he would let her stay in his house for as long as she wanted.

The next day, Abby was back with a mop and pail and cleaned the entire room from top to bottom. Even Brenner had to admit that it looked better.

Brenner was pleased that Abby had pretty much left things as they were. He liked how his room looked before, but was even happier with the way it looked now. He was only sorry that she had worked so hard and that he couldn't help her with any of her tasks.

Two days later, Elizabeth called her daughter to see how she was doing. They chatted for a while and got caught up on city news.

Pleased that things were going well and that her daughter was keeping busy, Elizabeth said, "I love you and will call you again in a few days."

"Thanks, mom!"

CHAPTER EIGHT

Two weeks after she moved in, Abby invited her sister and niece over to see how the place was shaping up. She was thrilled when they made a plan to come out. As soon as she hung up the phone with Melissa, Abby heard someone knocking on her front door.

"Coming!" she called. She stood up and ran curiously to the front entrance.

"Nick!" she shouted with much surprise as she opened the door to greet him. "How nice of you to come."

"These are for you." With one hand behind his back, he held the other one out to offer her a beautiful bouquet of assorted flowers.

Abby blushed. "They're beautiful! Thank you." She took them from his hand while inviting him inside. "It's a bit different than the last place, eh?" she announced while making a sweeping motion with her free hand around the room. She watched the officer as he looked around and touched everything in his path.

"Kinda spooky in here, don't you think?" He was commenting on the air, the mustiness, and the weird feeling inside the room.

Abby's eyes looked around the immediate area. "I guess, but it's home for me now. I'll get used to it." She sat down and hoped he would get the clue.

Nick walked around a bit more, looking at old things that were left behind by the previous owners, before he took a seat. "So, are you almost moved in?" he asked, now giving his whole attention to Abby.

Abby's turn to look around. "No. I still have a lot more to do before this becomes my home."

Brenner came down when he heard a man's voice. He was becoming nosy and had been trying to listen to their conversation pretty much the whole time. He didn't know who this guy was, but he didn't like him. What did he want with Abby, he wondered. And who was he to her?

"But what you've done so far, is pretty cool", Nick offered. He was commenting on how she mixed her things with the previous owner's items.

Abby's eyes scanned around the room again and she was feeling pretty proud of herself. "Thanks."

Brenner watched as the two adults sat on the couch and talked. Brenner listened as Nick told Abby about his job and then Abby told him about her move. Then, when the aura in the room took on a different shift, Brenner took more of an interest in the conversation.

"So, I was wondering if you'd ever like to have dinner with me sometime." Nick's breathing became shallow as he waited for an answer.

Abby bent her head with embarrassment. "Nick", she began slowly while playing with her hands which were lying in her lap. "You know that Casey has just died. I don't know if I'm ready to start dating yet."

Suddenly Nick was the embarrassed one. "Oh, don't worry", he lied while waving a floppy hand in the air. Nick had to think fast. He really wanted to be with her but didn't want to chase her away.

"I wasn't asking you to be my girl or anything", he laughed. "I just thought we could get to know one another and see where that would lead. You know, something light."

Abby was relieved but wasn't sure how to answer or

respond. Thinking dinner would not hurt, she agreed, but they couldn't decide on a time or date, so they left it open for the moment.

"Good enough." Nick was delighted with her answer. He reached into his wallet and pulled out what looked like a business card. "Here are my cell and home numbers. When you decide when you want to go out, give me a call." With that, he stood up and made his way to the front door.

"I don't want to rush you into anything, Abby", he said quickly as he turned back in her direction. "I just want to get to know you. I think you're a sweet girl and that maybe things could work out between us. I'm happy to leave it all in your hands."

Abby took the card and pressed it to her chest. "Thank you", she said. "Give me a few weeks."

"No worries." Nick was then gone as quickly as he had arrived.

Brenner couldn't have been more pleased. He wanted so much to ask Abby who that man was, but how could he lay rights to her when they haven't even met yet?

Abby put the card in the kitchen drawer for safe keeping and started straightening up the living room.

Abby put the flowers in a lovely vase that she had found in the kitchen, and filled it with luke-warm water. She set the entire item in the middle of the dining room table, fluffed up the flowers one more time, and then stood back to admire the whole thing.

After checking the time, Abby could see that her sister

and niece would be arriving in the next hour. She kept herself busy by unpacking.

After Echo said hello to Abby and commented nicely on how she liked what her aunt had done with the place, Echo then ran to find her male friend.

Melissa could feel something abnormal in the room, just like the before. Now she was convinced that it wasn't just a coincidence. She then remembered the last time when she was here, seeing a male figure in the upstairs window just as the car was pulling away.

She turned to her sister to see what she could find out. "So, has anything strange happened to you while you've been here?" She waited with bated breath until Abby answered.

Abby turned to her sister in surprise. What did she know, she wondered. Should she tell Melissa about Officer Nick? Abby's face went flush and she lowered her eyes as she decided to keep him to herself. "No, why?" Abby offered gently, not really knowing what Melissa was getting at.

Melissa wasn't sure if she should say anything further. She didn't want to scare or upset her sister if everything was going well.

"Nothing really", she commented, trying to sound nonchalant. "You're in a new place with new things around you. I was just wondering is all." Melissa tried to keep it light and non-threatening. Then she saw the flowers on the table. She wasn't sure if she should comment or not, so she kept quiet but knew that something was up.

Abby turned and paid no attention to what Melissa was really trying to say. With a more forceful voice she stated,

"As I said, nothing has happened. I've been alone and things have been very quiet." She let out a huge sigh of disappointment to the fact that she was lonely without Casey by her side.

Melissa saw the dejected look on Abby's face and decided to change the subject. She stood up and checked out how her sister had re-decorated her new home, touching a few of the petals on the newest addition in the room as she spoke.

"These are lovely." She turned to see if Abby would volunteer any information.

Abby lowered her eyes towards her lap. She wasn't about to confess anything pertaining to Nick just yet. She wasn't even sure if there was anything to say where he was concerned.

Seeing that her sister was not going to fess up, Melissa commented on a couple more things before she sat down beside Abby and got caught up with the latest gossip.

Brenner knew that Echo was in the house and that she could see him clearly. He tried to hide from her while he spied on the two women.

Melissa could not shake the feeling that someone was watching them. Then she came up with an idea. "Because this house is so old, wouldn't it be fun to have a séance in here?" She clapped her hands together while she waited for Abby to agree.

Abby slowly looked around the room and thought it might be a good idea, but was scared at the thought that a ghost would be living in the same house as her. There was indeed an odd coldness to the home, but that's not strange. It's an old house after all, she conceded.

"What if someone does live here and we don't know", Melissa said in a scary voice while her fingers curled in the air to frighten her sister.

"Stop that!" Abby shouted. She was getting spooked but believed in her sister's power of speculation. She slowly scanned the room again with her eyes. "There definitely is an unexplained coldness in here though, right?" She turned back to Melissa's face. "I guess it couldn't hurt, and it just might be fun."

"Yeeaah!" Melissa shouted as she smacked her hands together with pure joy. She hadn't been part of a séance in a long time and couldn't wait to get started.

Abby then sat back and wondered if this was such a good idea afterall.

Brenner listened to their conversation and laughed to himself about the séance, but knew that he would play along when the time came.

"Caught ya!" Echo yelled playfully once she finally found her friend from before.

Brenner jumped and then turned around to hush the little girl. He placed his index finger to his lips and tried to make a sound, but nothing came out. He didn't worry as he knew that Echo would understand what he was trying to say.

Echo watched her friend as he tried to hush her. She wondered why he was spying on her mom and aunt. She peeked around the corner and then saw that they were in the middle of some heavy-duty talking, which she didn't want any part of.

Echo reached up and pulled on his shirt. "Come on", she insisted. "Play with me like before."

Brenner couldn't believe that Echo could transcend over the two worlds. His shirt actually felt like it was being tugged on.

When it looked like he didn't want to play, Echo pouted and stamped her feet while she crossed her arms. "You're no fun anymore!" she whined. Then she turned and marched away angrily.

Brenner didn't know what to do. He wanted to stay and continue listening to the women's conversation, but he also wanted to be friends with the only human who has seen him in centuries.

He moved his head as he heard his little friend run away. Then he diverted his attention back to the ladies, but the more he heard coming from the beautiful young child, the more he wanted to be with her.

Brenner listened for another few seconds and then conceded that their conversation wasn't as much fun as playing with Echo. He made his choice to walk away.

Echo was well down the hallway when she felt Brenner's presence behind her. She turned and smiled and, after formal introductions, they played together for the rest of the afternoon.

"Because we don't know for sure if someone is really here or not, and we know nothing of this individual, we can hold the séance on any date", suggested Melissa. "If we knew who the person was that we're trying to contact, well, that changes things dramatically."

Abby knew that her sister had dabbled in wish craft and magic since she was a teen, so she probably knew something about séances as well. Abby trusted her sister where these things were concerned so she gave Melissa the green light to begin the process.

Melissa was thrilled and couldn't wait to start planning. She shifted her weight in the chair and suddenly everything about her face and demeanor came alive. Her voice was projecting with happiness and her hands were flying all around in front of her.

Melissa carried on. "It must be done at night, between the hours of 11:30pm and 12:30am preferably, because there is less interference from outside influences. In the daytime, everything from planes, television, and phone calls, to traffic going by can cause serious interruptions in the concentrated thought process necessary to séance successfully."

Abby listened and nodded in agreement, even though she didn't know quite what Melissa was talking about. It sounded correct though, she decided.

Melissa suddenly got up and started walking around a few rooms, continuing to speak and inspecting things along the way. She spread her fingers out in front of her like probes, trying to get vibes from different areas of the room. "We'll need an oval table, a large white candle, and an object from someone that used to live here."

Abby was mesmerized and stood up to follow behind her sister. Abby scanned the room as they walked, and looked at all the items that were scattered around her new home.

Within a minute, she had picked up something that she thought could work.

Brenner stopped frolicking and peeked around the corner when he heard footsteps coming towards where he and Echo were playing.

He gulped hard when he saw that what Abby had picked up, was an art piece that he had made for his mother so long ago. He hoped that Abby would treasure it and hold it dearly as both his mother and he had for so many years.

Watching Abby inspect the art piece, instantly transported Brenner back to the day when he gave it to his mother, and it made him miss her more.

Since he could remember, Brenner had watched his mother knit and sew, create and produce all the things that the family sold in their little store. One day, while he watched his mother sort her things on the table, he asked if he could try to make something himself. He didn't tell his mother that once it was made, he would present it to her as a gift.

"Of course you can make something", she chimed proudly. "Pick anything you want and make it work for you." She lovingly patted her son's head as she walked by him to go to the other room.

Brenner beamed with happiness at the thought of creating something for his mother. He looked at everything over and over again. He studied all the items that sat on the table and tried to think of something to make. When he focused on the white clay figurine near the back, he knew that this was what he could decorate and then give to his mother as a birthday gift.

Brenner found the paint, grabbed a few ribbons and some small pieces of material, and went off to a corner to work in private.

He struggled quite a bit and made a huge mess in the process, but eventually he was able to walk towards his mother with a gift that he hoped she would treasure for the rest of her days.

How proud Lilliana was of her son that day. She watched as his little legs walked towards her and then he handed his mother the small figurine that she had cast out of clay only a few days before. He had painted it, decorated it with colored cloth and ribbons, and had his father help him with the writing on the bottom......

To My Mother,
From your loving son,
Brenner

Lilliana shed a tear of joy as she held the object close to her bosom. Her eyes were clouding up with salt water as she watched her little boy climbing up and onto her lap to give her a hug with his tiny arms. "Happy birthday, mama", he whispered close to her ear.

Brenner's private moment was broken by Melissa's voice.

Melissa took the object from Abby's hand and inspected it by turning it upside down and around to the other side. "Yes, it really is lovely. This could definitely work." She placed it back down so that it would be easily accessible later.

"When did you want to have the séance?" asked Abby. She was watching her sister walk around the room touching this and that, and didn't want to wait too long to find out if there was someone else in the house with her.

Without turning around or making eye contact, she replied. "How does Friday night sound to you?" She wanted to do this as soon as possible and knew that they would be able to stay up late afterwards and talk until dawn. Even if nothing happened, it would be a great night for them to bond again.

Abby thought about it and then quickly agreed. "Wonderful!" she shrieked. She was scared but very happy that the séance would be done sooner than later.

Abby then had a thought. If someone was in the house with her, could it possibly be Casey, she wondered. She turned to Melissa and asked. "Could we pose a question during the séance?"

Melissa was pleased that Abby was on board now. "Of course a question can be asked", she offered. "What would you like to know?"

Abby became shy. "Don't laugh", she said harshly. "But I'd like to know if maybe, Casey is here with me." Abby watched as Melissa rolled her eyes and let out a sarcastic puff of air.

"The guy was a scumbag!" she shouted as her eyes went back to their original position. And then she thought about the question again. There was definitely someone or something in the house with them. Maybe it *was* Casey coming back from the dead.

Melissa turned to Abby. "Of course we can ask that question." Melissa also wanted to know the answer.

Abby was relieved. "Thank you", she answered as the

air softly released from her lungs. Her hands went into a prayer pose but the finger tips pointed away from her body. Then she watched as her sister picked up their stuff and was preparing to leave.

Melissa reached over and placed one hand on top of Abby's. "You are so welcome." Melissa removed her hand just as quickly and sat up. She started gathering her things from around her. "We should probably go as I now have a lot to do before Friday."

"Must you go so soon?" Abby loved having company, especially Melissa's.

"I'm afraid so." She turned her body as if she had radar, to tune in to where her daughter was playing. "Echo! Time to leave!" called Melissa.

Echo was disappointed that her time with Brenner was done. She stopped playing and bid him good-bye with promises that she would come back soon. Then she ran to her mother's side.

Brenner was sorry to see his friend leave, but also wished for her to come back soon.

The women said their good-byes and bid each other well until Friday night. Melissa took her daughter's hand as they walked towards the car. Then she remembered the last time that she stood by her small vehicle at Abby's new home.

After strapping Echo into the car seat, Melissa stood up and looked towards the upstairs window. There he was again. The same male figure.

"Melissa?" Abby called. She watched as her sister turned into a statue. There was a blank stare that presented itself all across her sister's face and she wasn't moving. "Are you alright?"

Melissa couldn't tear herself away from the window that easily this time. "Y-yeah. I'm okay", she said slowly. She blinked hard to release the hold that the man had on her, and then fixed her gaze on her little sister. "I am just fine", she kind of repeated.

Echo, who was watching her mother's face drop, sat up and looked towards the upstairs window of the farmhouse. There was her friend, just as before. She smiled and waved at Brenner and this time he waved back.

Brenner watched as both mother and daughter looked up and into his bedroom window. He knew that the daughter was able to see him, but now he wondered about the mother. It was eerie how she stared at him, like she could really make him out.

"Drive safe!" Abby commanded as she waved to the car that hadn't started rolling away yet. She took a few steps backwards and closer to the house. "Bye!"

Melissa got inside and put the car into gear, then looked into the back seat at her daughter. She saw that Echo had placed her body into the proper position for a drive. Now her headset was being placed on her ears, and in a minute she'd be napping.

"Ugh", Melissa moaned while smiling. "It's nice that some things will always be normal", she sighed.

CHAPTER NINE

Abby called her mom a day after Melissa's visit and filled her in on what would be happening on Friday night.

While supporting Melissa's knowledge in wish craft, but not into the whole séance and magic thing herself, Elizabeth wanted to be there with her children but could not due to work. Her company needed her in Montreal on the week-end, but she'd be back home on Monday afternoon. She expressed hope that Abby would fill her in with the major details when she got back.

"I will mom."

They spoke for another little while before Abby blessed her mom with a safe trip and then both said good-bye.

The next few days went by without incident. Brenner watched as Abby touched and moved things in his home, practiced her cello, watched TV, and cooked when needed. He was especially fascinated by the TV because he didn't know about this magical device before now. He wondered if the day would ever come when he could do these things with her.

Melissa and her daughter showed up just after 6pm on Friday night. Echo went off to play the second they came through the door, without giving any thought to what the grown-ups were going to be doing for the next little while.

Abby and Melissa started setting the scene for the séance in the living room, by the wall closest to the kitchen. "It has the most energy in the room", Melissa claimed.

The two girls dragged the large oval wooden table from its original spot, to the area which was chosen for it to sit. A dark colored cotton cloth covered it to the floor on all edges. Three chairs were placed around it: One for Melissa, one for Abby, and one for Echo.

Two large white candles were placed on the table and lit. One sat on the north side of the table, and the other on the south. The art object from the previous owner was laid in the middle in hopes that, if someone was here with them, he would appear sometime during the séance.

"I'll draw the curtains", Abby offered as she walked towards the large living room window. She had watched enough television to know that the room had to be somewhat dim when a séance was being performed.

Melissa smiled and nodded at the kind gesture. She was pleased that her sister believed in what was she was doing.

Once everything was set up, Echo was called from where she was playing.

Melissa had instructed her daughter about what was going to be happening at Auntie Abby's home that day, so she was quite versed on what to expect.

"Echo?" The second she heard her name being called, the little girl stopped what she was doing and ran to her mother's side.

They were instructed on where to sit and then they all sat down. Abby and Echo watched as Melissa lovingly placed a Bible in the middle of the table beside the art object. "This is to draw good spirits towards us", she stated matter-of-factly.

Abby looked at Echo to see her reaction to what was happening. She was surprised that her niece was content on just watching and learning from her mother.

Echo loved being in her mother's company for any reason, but when she did the odd séance or read someone's fortune, this intrigued her even more. She loved the energy in the room during those special moments and couldn't wait until she grew up so she could be the one conducting and conjuring.

Confident that if Echo was not scared or worried, then neither should she be. Abby then turned back towards Melissa who had just asked them to join hands.

Brenner moved himself towards that end of the house to see what was going on.

"Okay now, listen and learn", Melissa proclaimed in an authoritative voice. Her eyes went from Abby to Echo as she spoke. She needed both of them to totally understand and adhere to the rules.

"No-one is to speak until the very end. The spirits need only to hear one voice, and that is mine." She paused for effect.

"No-one is to laugh or rejoice in any manner. The dead cannot laugh and therefore levity offends them." She paused again.

"Do not break the connection or move your hands. Focus solely on my words and anything that you hear around us."

Abby started to get nervous as this was all starting to sound very serious. Abby didn't want any loud noises or things to go bump around her. What if I sneeze, or worse, cry, she wondered. Did she still have time to call this off?

With a soft smooth voice, Melissa continued with the

rules. "Now we shall close our eyes and keep our thoughts open." Melissa tugged on Echo's small hand as a reminder for her to behave and follow directions.

Brenner came closer. He watched and listened not far from where the three girls were gathered around his mother's table. He knew he had to stay out of Echo's immediate area so she wouldn't sense he was there and give him away.

"Let us begin."

Brenner moved a little bit closer so he could hear what was being said, while Abby took a deep breath and held it deep within her body.

"We are gathered together tonight, to invite the entity living in this home, to join us. Appear before us now. Show us that you are friendly. That you will not cause us any harm. We ask this with total respect."

Melissa, keeping her eyes closed and her ears open, waited for a moment to feel if there was anything different in the room. When she felt a slight change in the temperature, she began again.

"Tap once if you are friendly."

Brenner laughed to himself and decided to have some fun. He looked for something to knock against. He found a door within his reach and tapped it.

Everyone gasped, except Echo who knew in her heart that it was her friend trying to be silly.

Melissa opened one eye when she heard the knock, and looked towards Abby. Abby had also opened her eye to look towards her sister. They were both a little surprised until they looked towards Echo and saw that she had a smile on her face.

Melissa squeezed Echo's hand which made Echo look into her mother's worried face. She saw the look of concern and smiled. Forgetting the strict rules for a second, Echo spoke. "It's okay mother", she said. "It's only my friend."

The two sisters turned to each other almost simultaneously. "Told you someone was here," Melissa suggested as she looked in Abby's direction.

Abby's mind then flew to the day when Echo said 'he's silly'. Abby turned to the little girl. "You actually see someone in my house?"

Echo chuckled. "I not only see my friend in your house, I get to play with him", she replied.

Brenner got a chuckle out of the moment and waited for the next request.

Abby wasn't sure that she wanted to continue anymore but Echo squeezed her hand, a sign of confidence that it was okay.

"Ask him how come he's here, mommy", she whispered.

Melissa wondered the same thing. She gathered her thoughts, closed her eyes, and concentrated again. Knowing that she could only ask yes or no questions, she had to pose the question in that manner. "Are you here against your will?"

Brenner thought about the question and became sad. He took his own life and then couldn't leave, so yes, he was here against his will. He made a fist and tapped the door again.

Abby let out a rather obvious gasp. She felt Melissa squeeze her hand and then tried to recover.

Melissa continued as this was now getting interesting. "Tap once if you are a male."

"He's my boyfriend so yes he's a man", Echo added. She finished her sentence at the same time that Brenner tapped on the door.

Brenner chuckled to himself at Echo's comment. He hadn't been anyone's boyfriend in a very long time.

"Are you friendly?"

Brenner tapped once as he heard Echo chuckle to herself.

"He's friendly and silly", she added.

Brenner was pleased that he had made a friend.

"Is your name Casey?" Melissa inquired.

Brenner didn't know who that was so he tapped twice for no.

Both Melissa and Abby turned to look at each other. "Now what?" Abby asked.

Melissa continued. "Will we ever get to know you?"

Brenner had to think about that one. So far, he's only made contact with the little girl. He would like to make contact with Abby so he knocked once.

Abby took another gulp of air. What if he appears before me when I'm alone, she wondered.

This was too much for her so she moved her foot closer to Melissa's and stepped on it. She dug her heel into the barely clad toes of her sister, hoping that she would now put an end to this séance.

Melissa opened one eye and after seeing the scared expression on her sister's face, decided not to push things any further. She agreed to end what she was doing for today.

"We thank you for your presence and look forward to hopefully meeting you in the future." Melissa formally ended the séance, much to Abby's delight.

Melissa opened her eyes and bid the other two to do the same. She released her hands from the others as she blew out the candle and asked her daughter to open the curtains. The séance was now completed and they had learned a lot. Melissa felt that the whole thing went very well.

Abby moved away from the table and sat down on the nearby couch. She felt exhausted, drained of all energy and feeling terribly confused. Her thoughts were flowing with what had just happened, and she wondered when this 'meeting' was going to happen. Would she be alone, she wondered. Would it be frightening for her?

Melissa could see that her sister was becoming distressed. She came and sat beside her while she shooed her daughter to go and play. "It'll be all right, sis", she said trying to be comforting. "Nothing was really going to happen. We don't even know if this was fake or coincidence."

Melissa knew better of course. From what she saw in the upstairs window, from the manipulated manner of knocking, and the obvious joy that her daughter was getting while playing in this house, she could definitely guarantee that someone else lives here with Abby.

Abby turned and looked into her Melissa's eyes. "Promise?" she pleaded. Suddenly everything seemed rushed and unsure. Now she wasn't clear if what had happened was real. Maybe it was coincidental; the knocking and the slight coolness that went through the house during the questioning.

Melissa stroked her sister's hair repeatedly and wondered why she was so apprehensive. "Don't worry, sis."

Abby couldn't help it. Maybe someone *was* living in her home with her.

What Melissa felt was real. She knew it was a kind entity, one that would never harm anyone. But how could she tell that to a non-believer?

"Trust me, okay?" Melissa took her sister's face in her hands and touched their foreheads together. "It's going to be all right. I promise."

Abby wanted and needed to put all her trust into her sister's hands, but something held her back. She was truly scared, but why, she wondered.

"You okay now?"

Abby turned and looked into Melissa's smiling face. She hugged her sister and then knew Melissa was right. The whole evening had been just a bit scary for her. In the morning, things will be so much better.

"Yes. Thanks, Melissa."

The girls cleaned things up to the way the room looked earlier, and then put Echo to sleep in Abby's room. The sisters watched TV and talked for another two hours before Melissa admitted that she was getting tired.

The girls moved Echo onto the smaller couch while the bigger one was made up for Melissa. "Night!" Abby called over her shoulder as she left her sister's side.

Brenner watched Abby get ready for bed and then decided that it may be time for her to see him. Now he had to figure out how and when.

Brenner waited until Abby fell asleep and then crawled into bed behind her. As he looked into her kind face, he realized how truly beautiful she was. He pondered his future with her now that she lived in the house. Could they have one, he wondered.

Brenner turned to observe Abby as she moved, and then watched as she slowly fell into a steady rhythm of solid sleep. He felt sure that he now needed to show himself to her.

A few hours later, he left Abby's side to be close to Echo. He bent down close to the child's face and realized how fascinated he was by her mind.

"How is it that you can see me?" he asked his little friend, knowing full well that she was fast asleep. He gently stroked her small cheek and then left to go to his room upstairs.

CHAPTER TEN

Echo woke up first. She saw that her mom was sleeping peacefully on the long couch and decided not to wake her. Instead, she tip-toed off to find her friend.

Echo looked everywhere for Brenner but couldn't locate him. Sadly, she went back to the long couch and crawled under the blanket with her mother.

The movement stirred Melissa who was impressed to find her daughter so close. "Are you okay, my little one?" she asked in a playful, half-asleep tone.

Echo was sad because she couldn't find her friend, but didn't want to let on. "I'm okay."

Melissa hugged her daughter and playfully flooded her with kisses to her face and neck while she cooed soft, loving words to her ears.

Abby was stirring and could hear laughter in the next room. A smile immediately blossomed across her face as she realized that she was not alone. She rushed out of bed and ending up having a fantastic morning with her extended family.

The morning light makes everything look and feel different to ghosts, as well as to humans. Where last night he so wanted to show himself to Abby, this morning Brenner decided to leave well-enough alone. At least for right now. He would definitely give her his presence soon, but not today. Maybe he just needed to learn more about his new room-mate and her family before exposing himself.

As he stood up and stretched, pleased with his new decision, Brenner heard the enormous laughter bellow from the room below and came down to investigate. He peeked just behind the nearest wall, watching the three of them tickling each other and giggling with all their might. It gave him goose bumps.

The three girls played for another little while and then got cleaned up in time for breakfast. They were eating a hearty meal while Melissa and Echo decided what time they needed to leave, as the next day was for homework and laundry.

Echo was the first to finish her breakfast and then ran to find Brenner. They got to play for a very short while before their time was up. Just after the clock struck noon, they all said their good-byes and Melissa and Echo were walked to the car by Abby.

As usual, Brenner was in his bedroom watching them leave. He looked down and hoped that one day he would be able to be part of the good-byes, as well as the hellos.

Melissa stood by the car door and looked up at the window. She was not surprised to see the outline of a man standing there looking down. This time she waved to him and held her breath. He was the reason for the séance and she was pleased that he didn't fail her.

Echo moved her body forward in her seat. Her smile couldn't be wider as she saw her friend standing there watching her leave. She waved and silently wished him well, then sat back in her seat and waited for the car to be put into gear.

Brenner smiled and waved bye to both.

Melissa almost fainted when she saw him wave. The man was a like a white cloud but she could swear that he was smiling. She hoped that he now knew it was safe for him to come out of hiding.

Chapter Ten

Abby was oblivious to everyone saying good-bye to Brenner. She believed that the girls were saying good-bye to her. "Drive safe!" she called.

A moment later, Abby was alone again.

Over the next hour, Abby kept herself busy by cleaning and tidying up from the night before. After careful consideration, she decided that if someone was in the home with her, she might or might not ever really know. Until that day arrives, Abby will continue making the farmhouse her home.

*   *   *   *

Brenner watched Abby over the next two weeks and came to like her very much. Eventually the like turned to love and grew so strong that it consumed his every movement, motion, and thought. And this time, there was no-one around to forbid him to continue loving the woman before him.

He followed her around during the day and stayed close to her every night. As the days went by, Brenner got even closer to her. She was intriguing and well worth knowing.

Abby kept the séance in the back of her mind, but to date, nothing had ever happened. She was, by now, pretty confident that no-one was living there with her. This made her sad and happy at the same time. *She was sad that it wasn't Casey, and happy that it was no-one else.*

Abby chalked the knocking during the séance, up to mere coincidence and was learning to be content going through life alone.

*   *   *   *

Brenner watched Abby very closely one day, as she dashed around his bedroom, straightening this and tidying that. He loved how she glided with a kind of child-like quality, dancing to the music that was playing quietly in the background.

Abby finally finished the room to her liking. She was pleased with her efforts and decided to reward herself with a song. She realized that she had been neglecting her cello lately and softly scolded herself for it.

Abby walked peacefully to her music room and got herself ready to practice.

Brenner always made a point to be close when she played. He loved watching her strum her notes, and listened closely as she sang some of the songs.

Abby sat down and played a slow, romantic song on her cello. She hummed as she played, but broke down before the song was totally finished. Painful memories came flooding back of her and Casey in happier times.

They sat side-by-side in the dark theatre, chuckling at what was happening on the large screen before them. Casey leaned over and kissed her cheek quickly.

When Abby turned to look at him, he was facing the screen again and laughing at the antics of the main character as if nothing had happened.

Abby looked at his profile and couldn't take her eyes off of him. They had not had their first kiss yet. But what he did was innocent enough, wasn't it?

Abby turned back to the movie and tried to concentrate on what was happening in the plotline.

Ten minutes later, Casey leaned in to her nearest ear and asked her if she could do him a favor.

Abby couldn't imagine what he would need, but happily obliged. She was confused when he stood up and took her hand, helping her to stand up too.

Abby was surprised that she was now being guided to the hallway going out of the theatre. It was near the middle of the movie. What could he possibly want to ask her that couldn't wait until the end, she wondered. She didn't have to wait long before finding out the answer.

Casey led her towards the end of the very dark hallway that pathed between the lobby and the seating area where the other people were sitting.

He stopped and then gently leaned her back against the wall. He asked her again if she would do him a favor. She nodded yes, a bit frightened of what he was going to say.

"Don't be afraid", he whispered as his lips neared hers. In a single swoop, his mouth was on hers. The pleasure was only heightened because of the dark place that he had chosen to make this wonderful moment.

As his lips caressed hers, Abby felt his body move closer to her own. Casey's hands came up to her head, cupping her jaw on both sides. He leaned in a bit more and now his stomach pressed closer to her slim body.

Abby loved the feeling of him being so close. She wrapped her arms around his back and felt the soft fabric of his shirt, the bones and flesh underneath, and then rested her hands on his lower back where his pants were being held up by his belt.

Her head was swimming and she could hear that their breathing was both loud and hard. The only reason they needed to stop kissing was because a mom came through the double doors with her child, bringing light on the couple necking in the narrow space.

Casey smiled and giggled as he took a step or two apart from Abby, grabbed her hand, and then led her back to her seat. "Thanks for the favor", he whispered and then laughed out loud.

"That was the favor?" she chuckled not quite believing him.

He leaned his head closer to hers but kept his face towards the large screen. "I wanted to know what the connection would be if we kissed. The favor was you not pulling away."

They both laughed, returned their attention back to the screen, and enjoyed the rest of the show. When the movie was over, they held hands as they exited the large building. Abby turned to Casey's face and waited until he looked down at hers. Then she giggled, "Let me know when you want any more of those favors."

The month after that night, Abby found a class and started cello lessons because of that very movie. She learned how to play the theme music and it became their song.

Brenner watched as she cried and wanted to reach out and touch her. She was beautiful beyond any measure and he never wanted her to be sad.

Brenner tapped into her mind and found out the reason for her pain. He took a step backwards once it was revealed to him what had happened to Abby's fiancé. He knew that it was still fresh for her, but hated how it consumed her so often. He wished for the memory to go away, but how?

A distraction! Abby needed a distraction. Brenner moved himself into the living room. He closed his eyes very tight and concentrated on making himself whole. He then reached out and touched the small lamp beside the loveseat. Even he got scared when it moved and crashed to the floor.

Abby jumped out of her skin because of the loud sound and ran to the next room to investigate. When she saw the jagged pieces of glass on the floor, she became shocked. She had no idea how that could happen, or why.

She looked around the room and bravely called out, "Is anyone there?" She waited for an answer and then scolded herself for being silly. "Of course no-one is here."

Abby bent down and picked up the small pieces of the broken lamp and carried them to the garbage in the kitchen. She then cleaned up the larger pieces, checking to see what could be salvaged. Not much, but she would definitely be needing a new lamp.

Brenner was in disbelief. Had he really been able to move a solid object? He would try it again later to be sure. For now, he watched as Abby moved from one room to the other, cleaning up the mess that he had created.

When it was time for her to go to bed, he watched her as she got undressed. He had never done that before. He always waited until she was in bed before he came to her side, but tonight seemed different.

At first, Brenner became embarrassed, but curiosity got the better of him and he couldn't take his eyes off her beautiful form. As more and more clothing came off and she started stretching and moving about the room, he knew what he was doing was wrong.

Brenner made himself leave, even though he really didn't want to. It was well after midnight before Brenner trekked back to her room again.

He peeked inside and saw that she was now fast asleep, laying on her right side, facing the window. He came and stood beside the bed and listened to how she breathed. He gently lay down next to her and stayed there with her for the next few hours. He was fascinated with the fact that he cared so much for this person whom he didn't really know.

Over the next few days, Abby grew more suspicious. She felt like someone was watching her, even though she doubted her own mind. Was it just her nerves, she wondered.

Brenner started observing her more as Abbey's intuition heightened. He spied on her by creeping behind large objects, as if she would catch him if only she'd look in his direction.

More and more Abby thought that she could feel something strange, a pull of sorts, but that was impossible. She was there alone and she knew it, but somehow, it felt like there was someone else in the room with her.

After a while, Abby had had enough. She was now scared and making herself crazy. She had a thought. Abby went to the kitchen and pulled out the piece of paper with Nick's numbers.

Brenner followed her around with interest and then hated himself when he heard how scared she was.

"Hello?"

"Hi Nick, it's me, Abby." Abby held the receiver as if it were a life-line. It was dark outside and she didn't want to be by herself. Should she ask him to come over? She dared to ask.

Nick was delighted to hear from Abby. It had been so long since he had seen her that he had just about given up ever hearing from her again. "Have you decided on a date and time?" he inquired hoping that it would be in the near future.

Abby hadn't thought about their date. She was just scared and wanted to hear someone's voice. "N-no, I haven't, but I will", she fumbled. "I just thought it was my turn to say hello." Abby laughed at her poor excuse for a joke.

Nick was a bit crushed. He was hoping that maybe they had made a connection and that this was the phone call to start them dating. "Oh", he chided to himself.

Abby decided to come forward. "Nick, I think there's someone in the house."

Brenner's eyes closed tight immediately. He blew it. He was trying to stay close and all he did was spook her.

Nick's mind went on an immediate alert. All of a sudden, he was a cop and she was a victim. "Do you want me to come over and check things out?" he asked with hope in his heart.

"Would you be able to do that for me?" Abby's eyes were as big as saucers and her heart was now racing.

"I'll be right there." Nick kept his slippers on and threw the closest casual jacket over his arm. He grabbed his keys and out the door he went. He drove faster than he'd ever driven outside of a police vehicle, and arrived quicker than either Abby or Nick thought he would.

Brenner paid close attention to Abby as she waited on the couch for Nick to arrive. He watched her as she focused on every light that flickered outside of her home. He hated himself for making her so nervous.

Nick checked the farmhouse out from top to bottom, inside and out, while Abby followed closely behind him. They found nothing.

Abby was very relieved. She invited him in for coffee and they sat and talked for another hour before she felt better. Nick offered to stay longer but Abby assured him that she would now be okay. "Just nerves", she protested.

Nick left reluctantly, telling her that he'd call her the next morning.

"Thanks. I would appreciate that."

Abby went to bed, promising herself that she'd sleep with one eye open.

Brenner watched as Nick left and laughed coyly. He would never hurt her, but he wondered about the cop.

Brenner waited until she was fast asleep and then followed the hallway that led to Abby's bedroom. He walked in slowly and sat beside her as she slept. "I hope you know that I will never harm you." He then kissed the top of her head and closed his eyes.

She was pleased when Nick called the next morning, just

as he had promised. Abby asked him over for coffee and they sat and talked until noon.

Brenner didn't like Nick. He wanted Abby for himself and felt that Nick was a threat.

Nick loved his time with Abby. She was happy this morning and more wonderful than he had dreamed. He left her home with promises that they would finally make a date for dinner.

"I promise", she said while they were hugging good-bye.

Brenner watched and decided that maybe now was a good time for him to appear before her. The timing had to be just right though, or it could be even more disastrous for him.

After saying good-bye to Nick, Abby called her sister for advice and to fill her in on the night's adventure. Abby listened as Melissa told her how strongly she believed that someone was living in the house with her. She also guided Abby not to be afraid, just cautious.

"Easy for you to say", she chuckled. Abby was trying to be funny but she was shaking and wanted to cry.

They talked for another little while before Melissa promised to come by on the week-end for another visit. They would talk more then.

Abby thanked her and hung up. She now became more in tune with the old farmhouse and its eccentricities. Since speaking with Melissa, Abby felt more aware that someone could be living in the house with her. She was alert but not worried when she heard strange noises, or when the climate changed from room-to-room.

Abby was watching TV right after supper when she heard

a sharp noise coming from the hallway opposite the front door. She wanted to go and check it out, but decided that it was her mind playing tricks on her again.

A few minutes later, the noise came again only louder and closer. Abby became frightened now. Should she call Nick again, she wondered.

Before Abby could reach the phone, she felt an odd coolness envelope her with more love than she'd ever felt before. She was warm inside, at peace, and not afraid at all, but staggered with curiosity about what was happening.

The TV turned off which made her eyes become as big as saucers while her mind and body were searching for clues as to what was going on in the room. Off in the corner, Abby saw something move and it held her attention. Could it be?

Brenner decided that tonight was the night. He stood in the far corner and waited. He would only go as far as she could handle and then he would stop when she's had enough.

Abby was terribly intrigued now while still a bit frightened. "Is someone there?" she asked with trepidation in her voice. She didn't want an answer but she still wanted to know,

"I'm here", he said slowly and methodically through mental telepathy. The tone of his voice was calming and tender.

Abby heard a soothing voice in her mind. It then dawned on her that whoever was living there with her, wanted to make contact. Should she let it happen, she wondered.

She was all alone and now becoming nervous. Would she be able to do this by herself? Should she?

"Will you hurt me?" She choked back a tear as she spoke out loud. She gathered the small couch blanket closer to her body while her eyes scoped out the room around her.

"No, not at all", he said again through mental telepathy. He knew now that she could hear him loud and clear. "Do you want to see me?"

Abby wasn't sure that she wanted to continue. Was her mind playing tricks on her, she wondered. Was this real, or her imagination. She looked around the room for a clue to her sanity.

Abby blinked and nodded her head while trying to release the scary thoughts from her brain. She picked up the control and tried to turn the TV back on but it didn't work.

Brenner waited patiently while Abby thought about her answer. He could feel the turmoil going through her body and mind and didn't want to rush anything. If tonight was not going to be perfect for her, he would certainly wait for another time.

Abby suddenly became angry with herself. She needed to stop being a child. She pushed the blanket away roughly as if to make a statement. "If someone is in here with me, show yourself", she demanded. "I'm done being afraid." She gulped down her fear and put her chin up to face the music. Her eyes continued to scan the room for another weird or strange occurrence.

Brenner watched her as she spoke. He loved her spirit but

wanted to make sure that she really was ready for what was about to happen.

"Are you still here?" she asked quietly while trying to be brave.

Brenner clenched his fists tightly and stood his ground as a strange light shone all around him. Little-by-little, parts of him went from white and not there, to slowly coming into focus. He watched Abby's expression the whole while and knew that he would stop if she wanted him to.

Abby's eyes widened and her heart quickened as she watched a man slowly appear before her. He was very handsome, tall, dark, and his presence seemed friendly enough. He didn't say a word but appeared spectacular and refined.

Brenner's body felt fizzy as it became more whole. He hadn't made himself visible for a very long time and wasn't even sure if he knew how anymore. He did what he remembered and hoped that it would work.

Abby was full of wonderment when she saw this gorgeous man appear before her. Her heart was pounding in her chest and her body wanted to run quickly out of the room, but something kept her tied to her spot on the couch.

Brenner loved that Abby was still interested in what was happening. "Are you still okay?" he asked her mentally. His voice was gentle and alluring.

Abby sat up straighter and placed both feet firmly and squarely on the floor before her. "I think so", she began. She was now more intrigued than she could imagine. This was more surreal than she could explain, but she knew it wasn't over yet.

"Who are you and why are you here?" she asked out loud, bewildered by what the answer would be. She wished that her heart would slow down but it couldn't out of fear.

Brenner was now totally in focus but knew that he still needed to be cautious with her.

"My name is Brenner Jaxon."

CHAPTER ELEVEN

After the introductions were made, they sat across the room from one another and started to ask questions about the other person's life. They ended up talking all night long, and soon were sitting side-by-side on the same green couch by the window.

By the end of the night, they had slowly learned who each of them were: where they came from and how they came to be in the farmhouse. Both were fascinated by the other's lives. Both were feeling a great deal more comfortable and protective of each other, especially after learning about the other's past.

Abby's fears about Brenner and the unknown were long gone by the time the morning sun shone through the windows. She was feeling very comfortable with him by the time the birds started chirping for their breakfast.

It surprised Brenner to feel as close as he did to Abby after only just speaking with her for a few hours. Of course, it didn't hurt that he had watched her in his home for weeks now.

Abby was very surprised to learn that Brenner had never ventured outside of the solid frame of the old farmhouse. She suddenly had a thought. "Do you mind if I show you something?" she inquired.

Brenner couldn't imagine what she could show him that he wouldn't have already known about his home. "Of course", he announced with a dare in his voice. He placed a smirk on his face and bowed his head as he used his hand in a 'show-me-the-way' manner.

"Okay, follow me", she instructed.

While a bit unsure if he would want to see what she had

to show him, she decided that he probably would. Abby gracefully stood up, as if she was a ballerina in mid-dance, and motioned for Brenner to follow.

Brenner was mesmerized by her. He watched Abby as her gorgeous foot sprung forward, toes pointed, and then landed softly on the dark wooden floor. Her eyes sparkled and her lips turned up at the edges, somehow making everything in the world seem perfect. Of course he would follow her anywhere.

Abby moved across the floor like an angel until she reached the foyer and stopped. She glanced over her shoulder to see if Brenner was still following.

Brenner was definitely right behind her. He had seen the outside from the windows, but he had never ventured out into the open air in the entire lifespan of his death.

Abby opened the front door and then stood at the doorway and looked out towards the yard. She took a step outside and looked back, keeping an eye on Brenner's face and expression. She saw that he was hesitant at first, but then he put one foot in front of the other and soon he was standing on the old front porch of his youth.

Brenner was suddenly full of emotion. His heart swelled and he could feel goose bumps all over his body. He looked down and saw that his very own two feet were standing firm and flat on the old wooden floor boards which he and his father had nailed together so long ago.

The grand old vestibule was a great pride to Brenner's mother. She held many an afternoon tea on this old porch, talking and laughing with her friends and neighbors.

Brenner looked over at Abby and was overcome with

emotion. "Thank you", he said silently as he tried to fight back the tears. A flood of memories exploded in his mind.

Abby squeezed her eyes shut tightly and smiled. "There's more." She started to walk down the steps then turned to see if he would join her.

Brenner was overwhelmed but started following right away. He was filled with wonderment at all that he could see and smell. He tried to guess where Abby was leading him but couldn't take his eyes off the scenery.

Abby stopped a few feet from a large weeping willow tree that stood very close to the edge of the property. She waited patiently for Brenner to catch up but knew that he had a lot to digest.

Abby watched as Brenner looked all around the fields, back at the house, to this side and that. After taking his time to inspect everything, he finally appeared at her side. She watched as he looked up to see how tall the tree, which he had planted as a young child, had grown. He had seen it from the large window, but to be actually standing underneath it again, that was something else.

Brenner placed his left hand against the rough bark, his fingers finding the curvy crevices, and he wanted to cry. His head fell forward from his body and then he noticed the two tombstones. "Why hadn't I seen these before?"

He turned back and looked quickly towards the farmhouse and back again. Then he knew. The graves were facing east and were hidden from his view from the house because of the tree.

Abby watched as Brenner slowly removed his hand from

the tree. In a mourning, somber state, he moved closer to where his mother and father had been laid to rest.

Brenner, on bended knee, placed one hand very lovingly on top of his father's headstone. He read the inscription to himself and wanted to cry. He looked up at Abby's face. "This is where they've been this whole time?" he asked.

Abby nodded and then it occurred to her that Brenner may not have known anything after he died. She suddenly felt very sorry for him.

Brenner turned again and looked at his mother's inscription. "She passed away shortly after I did", he stated. Brenner looked up at Abby's sad face again. "Do we know how they died?"

This farmhouse and property had been in Abby's family for years. At first, no-one knew who the two graves belonged to or how they died. Many trips to town to visit the library and City Hall, gave them the information that they needed. Once they had learned who these people were, the family decided to keep the couple buried there as a conversation piece. "This is where they lived, and this is where they'll stay", she heard her Uncle say once.

"I believe your mother died from influenza", Abby disclosed. "Your father was very distraught and couldn't function after he lost both you and your mother. It's believed that he died from a broken heart. He just gave up one day and was found in his bed by the lady who came in once a week to clean."

Brenner looked back at the two spots where his parents laid. He closed his eyes and said a few thoughtful words in his head. Then he kissed the open palm of his left hand and placed it lovingly on top of his father's tombstone. He did the same thing to his mother's and then stood up, his head bent forward.

Abby wished that she could comfort Brenner by rubbing his back or taking him in her arms. She knew that there was nothing she could do but offer him her condolences. "I'm sorry, but I thought you'd want to know."

Brenner had seen enough for one day. Without speaking, he turned and almost ran back to the farmhouse and up to his room. He needed a few minutes to himself and hoped that Abby would understand.

Abby felt the sad and confused vibes that he was sending her, so she let him be. She knew that he needed to be alone for a while to digest everything that she had just shown him. She also realized that it was a lot to process.

Abby leaned against her mid-sized vehicle and looked out at the vast surroundings. She breathed in the fresh air and held it inside her lungs. Then she slowly let it out while closing her eyes. She lifted her chin and let the sun heat up her face while she pondered about what to do next.

Abby took a few minutes to walk around the property and loved what she saw. She had so many questions about her new friend and his past, but knew they would have to wait.

Abby let Brenner have an hour or so to himself before she beckoned him again. She figured that if he could just show himself to her, she would know if he was okay.

She sat on the smaller couch, closed her eyes and opened her mind, and then Abby said his name while releasing a breath of air.

Brenner appeared within seconds and first apologized for running off, and then he thanked Abby for everything.

"Oh!" Her hand went up to her chest.

After her initial shock of seeing him when she'd just made a wish for his presence, Abby was glad for his company and then asked if he wanted to go further.

Brenner couldn't imagine what she meant. "You mean further than the front yard?" His eyes grew large and full of hope.

"Of course!"

Brenner didn't know what to say. He looked around the very familiar room and couldn't believe that he had spent this whole time cooped up inside of these four wooden walls. He turned back to Abby and nodded but didn't know how to thank her properly.

Abby watched as he came and knelt down beside her.

"I want to see and enjoy everything that you want to show me."

Abby was breathless. She loved how he spoke - his accent, the language, and the formality. She knew that he had come from a different time period and wished with all her heart that she could have been born into his lifetime. Maybe she could have even been his bride.

Abby looked deep into his eyes as her mind wandered.

"Are you okay?" he questioned when he saw the glazed look on her face.

Abby snapped back to reality quickly once she heard his voice in her mind. "Yes, yes", she replied. *I was just thinking of how wonderful it would be if only you were real.*

"We can go for a ride in my car tomorrow", she remarked. "I can take you all over this immediate area so you can see how it's changed."

Brenner marveled at the thought. He stood up and moved himself to the large window. "A car", he announced. "How does one learn to drive such a thing?" He turned back to Abby and waited for her to answer.

Abby was taken back. It had been years since she got her license and it was a bit of a blur to her now. "Well", she explained. "At the age of 18, you go and write a test. If you pass, you take driving lessons until you feel confident enough to be evaluated. When you are ready, someone evaluates you on what you think you know. If you pass, you get your license."

Abby was now fishing through her purse to find her wallet. Her license was under a small, clear, plastic window near the front. She held it up to Brenner so that he could see it. "Here! This is what it looks like."

"I see."

Embarrassed by the picture, Abby put the wallet back into her purse. "Once you have a license, you have to renew it every few years on the day of your birthday", she recited after moving her purse to the side.

"Amazing", he remarked.

Abby then realized how different their lifestyles had been. Everything that she had complained about while growing up, was nothing to how Brenner had to live. She had a flushing toilet in the bathroom inside the house, while he had to go outside where he sat on a cold, open hole in a wooden shelf. She had natural heat coming up from the vents in her home, while he had to gather wood to make a fire every night. She grew up with grocery stores, while he had to grow whatever he wanted to eat.

There were lots of differences and lots to learn from on both sides.

That night, they sat together and watched the flames in the old fireplace burn as they continued to talk for hours. At one point, Abby turned to Brenner and asked him about living in the farmhouse as a child.

Brenner had forgotten a lot over the years. He wasn't sure if it was because he had blocked it out, or because he hadn't thought about it for a while and it just got lost in his memory. He was pleased that when he started talking and remembering, it all came back as easily as when he had lived it.

Brenner Jaxon, an only child, was born in the old farmhouse two years after his parent's wedding. The house was small at first, but Mr. Jaxon added a second bedroom, extended the sitting room, and provided his bride with an updated, fancy kitchen.

Mr. Jaxon suggested that his wife could use the second bedroom as a work area. She could use it to sew, create, and display her wares before they were sold at their store.

Mrs. Lillianna Jaxon was delighted and immediately started to set the space up to her liking.

Mr. Jaxon was thrilled. He did everything in his power to make it dainty and delicate to suit his wife's needs and wants. An expensive two-seat, brightly-colored, hand-embroidered couch sat on one side of the room, and a very handsome, hand-made rocking chair on the other where Mrs. Lillianna Jaxon could sit and sew. There was also a long table near the window where she could spread out her many items to view or add other compliments to her pieces.

The large and airy top room over the kitchen was added years after the couple moved in. Mr. Jaxon knew that he would need to design and build a very suitable ladder for that room. The rungs were made larger and stronger than a regular ladder, which made things much easier for his wife to go up and down when catering to her child's needs.

The couple gave that room to Brenner and turned it into a bedroom/playroom when the boy was just 7 years old. It was then when Mr. Jaxon believed that it was high time that his son had his own space. Up to that point, the family had been sleeping in the same room.

Brenner helped decorate his room and loved that all the space was his very own. A large carpet was dragged upstairs and placed in the middle of the room, giving a one-foot wooden floor space between the rug and the exterior walls.

Brenner grew up in what some people would say as luxury, surrounded by 50 acres of well-developed land that sprouted everything from potatoes and corn, to live stock and flowers. His parents were able to supply products to people in many different counties and their money was ever-flowing.

On the edge of their vast landscaped property, was a quaint corner store where people from all around, would come and get their wares. Winters were a little harder to sell their grown products, so Brenner's mother knitted and sewed scarves, mittens, sweaters, and such all year round to keep their small store operating, and themselves in money.

Abby listened intently. She loved hearing stories about how people lived and survived in the past. "What was your mother like?" she asked, trying to keep him talking.

"Can I show you what she was like?" he asked extending his hand to help her up, even though he knew she couldn't take it. It was a game that they had played many times…. him being a gentleman, even bowing at times just to make her smile or laugh.

Abby got up, very curious in what he was about to show her.

Brenner walked her towards the kitchen. "Here!" He pointed towards the kitchen floorboards in front of the double sinks. "Open that one and see what's underneath."

Abby became intrigued and immediately went down on her knees, moved the woolen carpet aside, and tapped on the floorboards. She first found, then pried the loose floorboards from their foundation, and looked inside of the deep, dark space.

"I can count eleven jars of coins under here!" she exclaimed with powerful surprise. "Why hadn't anyone known about this before?"

"The small rug covered the spot where the money was hidden," he began. "Its main purpose was to provide a soft spot for someone to stand while doing dishes or making meals."

Abby lifted the 1-gallon jars out one at a time, placing them all around her on the kitchen floor. She couldn't believe her eyes. "Please tell me more."

Abby listened intently as Brenner regaled in the history of the money, and of his parent's lives.

Lillianna's family was desperately poor while she was growing up. When money started coming in from the farm and the store, she saw this as a gift from heaven. Mrs. Jaxon looked at her husband and child and then thought about their future. Of course she wanted the best for her family so from then on she knew what she had to do.

The very next day, Lilliana started saving for a rainy day by putting most of her change in a jar. She kept a bit for expenses, but the majority of the coins went under the floorboards. She never wanted to be poor again and thought that if things got bad, or if in the future things continued to prosper, they would always have enough money to live on.

Lillianna did this kind act out of love and never told another soul her secret.

Abby took a deep breath and sighed. "How fascinating!"

CHAPTER TWELVE

After Abby put the jars back where she found them, she continued to listen to Brenner speak while moving into a comfortable position. "Please, tell me more about your mom."

Brenner watched as Abby rolled over onto the right side of her body and squished a throw pillow to her chest. He loved how her face was lit up by the stories of his past and family. He also changed positions and then continued.

Lillianna had an arranged marriage and she was very frightened at first, but after meeting Charles the day before their wedding day, her fears had calmed and subsided. They were able to take a short walk, escorted by a housemaid, and talk about a few things before the ceremony.

A few minutes into their walk, Charles confided that he didn't care if he was married or not. He sarcastically stated how much he just wanted to get out of his parent's home. Charles liked Lilliana and how she looked, but he wasn't ready for the responsibilities of marriage. He felt that he was still too young to be tied down but didn't have a hope of arguing that point with his parents.

Since Lillianna had pretty much the same idea, she welcomed the thought of marriage to this stranger. She also liked the idea that he would not want anything from her, such as the silly things she had heard from her girlfriends down the road: Things that make them all giggle and get embarrassed.

The walk ended with both parties agreeing to be married in name only, and for the sake of their families. Both sets of parents were ecstatic, money was exchanged, and papers were signed. Everyone toasted the happy couple and then waited for the next day to arrive.

Charles and Lilliana toasted each other as well. They clinked glasses agreeing to be friends only while living together pretending to portray a married couple.

Their wedding ceremony, simple and quick, was performed in her parent's living room the day after the couple met. He was 25 while she was only 16 years old. Once the ceremony was over, the parents partied while the newlyweds were taken to the farmhouse to start their new life. They had their own little party of wine and moonshine, and danced around until the morning. They celebrated their freedom from their parent's rules, and were overjoyed by the new experience that lay ahead of them.

They didn't consummate their marriage until a year later. Neither was in a hurry and both were having too much fun being best friends to worry about starting a family or doing 'the deed'.

Lillianna and Charles were like teenagers having a sleep-over. Theirs was an easy relationship, no hang-ups or routines. They did what they wanted, when they wanted, and had no adult around to tell them otherwise.

One stormy night, almost 12 months to the day when they got married, the wind was howling and the pouring rain streaked the sky in thick, grey lines. They were in bed together talking and laughing, when a sensuous feeling stirred within Lillianna's lower body. A sensation that she'd never known before, but now wanted to explore.

Charles had been ready for this encounter for a few months but was waiting for his wife to make the first move.

Charles stopped talking when he saw the look in his wife's eyes. He saw her face coming towards him and his heart started pounding. Of course they had kissed before, but it was almost always on the cheek. When her lips touched his, he trembled but held back. He wasn't sure if he should reach out to her, or let her come on her own.

The kiss was incredible. She wasn't sure why she suddenly did it, but was immediately glad. She liked it very much and now wondered why they hadn't done it before. She kissed him again, only this time she didn't stop. She reached both hands up to his face and seemed to pull him closer to her body.

Charles couldn't stop what she had started. He kissed her many, many times and also wondered why they hadn't done this sooner.

Lillianna ripped the gown over her head while the adrenaline rushed through her body. She then watched as her husband sat up and took the clothes of himself as well. Now they were naked for the first time ever.

She watched him slowly getting on top of her exposed body. At first, Lillianna laughed at what was hanging down from between his legs. She reached out to touch it and was surprised when it grew harder in her hands. The feelings between her legs were now growing stronger.

Lillianna felt Charles put his hand over hers and then he helped guide her to where he needed to go. She was very surprised that while there was a bit of pain, there was a great deal more pleasure.

Charles went slowly at first, one inch at a time until he was completely inside of Lillianna's body. He watched her face below his as his hard and straightened member disappeared between her legs. He wanted to make sure that she was not in a lot of pain, as he had always been told would happen to a virgin.

Lillianna's thoughts cleared once the pain was gone. She loved the feeling of his body so close to hers, the sweat that poured off his brow, and the way his breathing changed with every beat of his body banging softly against hers.

All of a sudden the slow, steady rhythm changed and it became quick. Before she could utter a challenge, it was all over and Charles collapsed on top of her.

Lillianna smiled with the knowledge that she was now a woman and Charles was her true husband. She lovingly wrapped her arms around him and knew that she would cherish him for the rest of her life.

For the next few weeks, they experimented and had fun. While they didn't have these encounters every night, the times they did enjoy it, were more and more pleasurable. This added a new dimension to their relationship and made their love and friendship even stronger.

Over time, they decided that their days of fun and glory were done and it was time to be grown-ups. They talked and both agreed to make their farm work so they could earn their own money.

Once they figured how and the farm started producing, the money came in quickly. Lillianna knew that she needed to think of a way to put some away. It took her no time at all to come up with a plan.

The day after she was told that her new kitchen was now ready for her to use, Lillianna decided to take this opportunity to find a safe spot for their money.

She undid a few of the floorboards in front of the kitchen sink and dug away the dirt that laid directly underneath. She was ever so pleased that the soil was loose and easy to remove. Lillianna ended up making a hole big enough so that it would hold a great deal of money.

She started with just one jar and when it was full, it was placed under the floor boards. She was very proud of herself and continued filling more and more jars over the course of her lifetime.

Lillianna died first before ever telling her husband of the small fortune which she had hidden. He died a short while later without ever finding out what she had so lovingly done for their future.

Abby questioned Brenner why he didn't know about the money before now. She listened as he explained.

"I remembered the one and only time that I saw my mother put a jar away. I was only 4 years old. I came into the kitchen and stopped when I saw my mother down on her knees. The carpet had been pulled aside and she was putting something inside of the floor."

"What did she say to you?" Abby was breathless with anticipation.

Brenner laughed at how inquisitive Abby had become. "My mom got spooked when I came up behind her. When she heard me approach, she quickly dropped the jar inside of the hole and stood up, dusting off her knees and straightening the small carpet in front of the sink.

Once she recovered from being startled by me, she turned around and angrily hushed me to silence, making me swear never to tell a living soul about the money. She threatened me severely if I were to ever break this promise, so I never did, until now."

He looked into her kind eyes. "I actually forgot about the money altogether, until this very moment."

"So you kept your promise to your mother after all."

"I guess I did", he said shyly. Not thinking that it was such a big deal.

Abby wanted to muss his hair or playfully push him backwards, but couldn't because he was not real enough. This fact was beginning to bother her. She wanted to be able to touch him. Then it occurred to her, would he want to touch me too, she wondered.

"Do you regret dying?" she asked with trepidation in her voice.

Brenner looked at her with such confusion. "What kind of a question is that to ask?"

Abby became embarrassed. "I-I didn't mean anything rude", she began. "I meant, if you had to do it over again, would you .....?" She didn't know how to ask the question with dignity.

"Die?" he asked without fuss or concern.

Abby bowed her head in shame. She was now sorry that she had brought it up.

"I guess so", he replied after thinking about it. "I mean, what I did, was done so quickly and without much forethought. I wanted to stop my hurt by making someone else feel the pain. I wasn't thinking and you are right. I would not do the same thing again if I had the chance."

Abby still didn't know how he died, but after his response to her last inquiry, she decided not to ask. She now didn't know how to handle the next minute. Do I change the topic, she wondered.

Luckily, she didn't have to do another thing. Abby watched as Brenner slowly stood up and walked away.

"I'll be back", he said softly, and left. He needed time to think.

Abby waited for a little while and then realized that she had goofed and he was not coming back any time soon. Abby hated his bad habit of always running away, but she pried where she shouldn't have. Still, his death intrigued her.

Another hour had passed before Abby looked at the time. As she stood up and stretched, she contemplated that she would wait until the morning to talk with him again.

CHAPTER THIRTEEN

Abby woke up the next morning and called her sister right away. She told Melissa everything that her and Brenner had talked about the day and night before. She even told Melissa of a secret wish, if she could have one, of which Brenner was alive so that they could be together.

Melissa could hear sadness and doubt in Abby's voice as she spoke. "And why couldn't it happen?" Melissa rejoiced. With all her background in wish craft and magic, she was sure that it could be possible.

Abby blinked a few times and made a face. "Come on now! How is that possible?" While she had a faint doubt, a part of her mind wondered if it could really be done.

"Why not? With spells and wishes as strong as a heartbeat, some things can and are possible. You just have to want it bad enough."

Abby was quiet for a moment. She believed in her sister and her powers of persuasion. Could it really be possible, she asked herself. "I need to talk with Brenner. Can I call you back?"

"Most definitely."

Abby closed her eyes while thinking of his face and wished for Brenner to appear before her. She said his name slowly as she released a puff of air. Suddenly, she felt him close by and opened her eyes to see his form before her.

"You called?" he whispered softly. He loved it when she summoned him. It made him feel like a genie.

Abby smiled and asked him to sit down. "First, let me apologize if I was out of line before."

"You weren't", he sighed, embarrassed by his disregard for

her feelings when he runs off. "I just really wish I would have thought the act of suicide through, before I did it."

Abby couldn't imagine what he must be thinking, but wanted to follow-through on that same line of conversation. She discussed the possibility of him becoming human for a while. "Would you ever want to?" she asked. "I mean, if you could."

Brenner had to think, but not for too long. "I think I would, yes." The possibility was intriguing, but he knew not possible. He would go along with her quest for now, to see what she was up to.

"Great! I'll call my sister back and see what we have to do to make this work." With that, she was off to the nearest phone. She could feel that Brenner was right behind her.

Brenner knew that Melissa was special, that she could sense things that Abby could not. Was it possible that Melissa had a power to make him whole again, he wondered. Even for a little while? Brenner started to get excited at even the slightest possibility of that happening.

"He said yes!" she shouted into the phone for Melissa to hear. "Now what? Can you help, or do we need someone with more power?"

Melissa agreed that they would definitely need help from someone with more powers. She suggested that they talk to a clairvoyant, a soothsayer, an avatar. Melissa certainly made it sound like this was a done-deal and that it could really happen.

Abby, while still a bit skeptical, was blown away that this just might work.

Melissa came to the farmhouse a few days later with a ton of enthusiasm, but without Echo. Echo had a dance class and was then having a sleep-over at her friend's house. Melissa was on her own for the next few hours.

Abby sat Melissa down and then summoned Brenner to the room while Melissa watched with intrigue.

A second later, Abby smiled and then kind of introduces Brenner to Melissa.

Melissa could barely make out a form but felt something different in the room. A strange coldness and mustiness of the air arrived at the same time that Abby said Brenner was now in the room.

"How is it that I can see you in the upstairs window when I leave, but I can't see you here in this room?" she asked out loud to the air where she thought Brenner was standing.

Brenner smiled. He used mental telepathy to answer her question but both women could hear him clearly. "I am still shy around you, Melissa. I'm holding back a bit, but not from Abby anymore."

"Now, about your daughter. Echo seems to have no problem seeing, hearing, or touching me. It baffles me and I haven't quite figured that part out yet."

"My bedroom, well, that is my safe zone. I become as whole as I can be in that room. If you can see me from the window, it's because the power is the strongest in there."

Melissa could hear every word in her mind. She smiled in his direction and thanked him out loud. "I understand and won't push."

After the introductions, the three of them discuss everything about Brenner becoming alive.

After a while, they decide to move to another area of the house. They all huddled around the computer, punching in any words they could find (avatar, soothsayer, psychic, clairvoyant, fortune teller, etc…) until they were exhausted.

The one name that kept coming up on every website was, Destiny Allen. Apparently, she was the one and only person who had the power they were looking for.

"Dial!" Melissa shouted after all three agree that she's the one.

With Brenner's hand sitting lightly on her left shoulder, Abby punched in the phone number right away.

"Your Destiny awaits. How can I help you?"

Abby held her breath and wasn't sure how to reply.

Brenner saw her hesitation and prodded her on.

Abby felt his frustration and spoke up. "uh, Hi", she began. "My name is Abby and I would like to set up a meeting with Destiny."

The woman on the other end had a light voice. "Of course", she said. "When is convenient for you to come in?"

Abby wanted this to happen right away. "When is your earliest appointment?" she asked. "And do we come there, or do you come here?"

"Destiny can do either", she offered. "If you wait just a moment, I will put her on the line for you."

"Oh my!" Abby was both euphoric and scared. What

was she getting herself into, she wondered. Then she remembered Brenner and knew.

A wonderful voice came on the line, music playing softly behind her. "Hello, my name is Destiny. Would you like to meet tomorrow morning?"

Abby looked at Brenner and Melissa and watched as they both nodded their approval. "Yes, that would be just fine", she answered. "Would 9am be okay with you?"

"Actually, 9:30 would be better."

Abby didn't mind the extra half-hour. "9:30 on September 7 it is." With that, Abby thanked her for her time and they ended the call.

Abby and Melissa stood up, screamed, and danced around the room, hugging each other. Brenner was delirious with the prospect of finally being able to hold and love Abby like a man.

Abby ran to the phone and called her mom. "Are you interested in looking after Echo for an hour or so at my house tomorrow morning?" Abby could hear how happy her mother was and then explained that the two girls were going to get their palms read and their futures told.

"How exciting!" she beamed. Inside, she could tell that there was more to the story, but for now she'd go along with what she was being told.

Elizabeth had her own small amount of ESP, but kept her tiny powers to herself. Mostly what she had was precognitive clairvoyance – she could tell that something was about to happen and what it was in great detail, but it mostly pertained to herself. Her gift was no good for anyone else.

Elizabeth had mentioned it to some people in her lifetime, but they scoffed and said that she misunderstood what she had. They claimed she just had strong intuition. Some said it was pure nonsense and laughed.

Elizabeth, in time, decided to stop telling people about her gift.

"Of course I will babysit", she gushed. Elizabeth arrived 30 minutes before her daughters left the house so they could visit and get caught up. It wasn't often that Elizabeth had both her children in the same room at the same time. She wanted to enjoy every moment with them.

Echo loved her grama with all her heart but wanted Brenner to stay and play with her.

"You know I have to attend this meeting, right?" he whispered towards her beautiful face. "And we'll be back soon."

Echo listened as he spoke and made him promise to play with her when he returned. She watched as he smiled proudly at the request.

"I wouldn't want to do anything but", he replied.

Echo watched as her mother and Aunt Abby got into the car. She waved frantically as it pulled away from in front of the house, and then she turned her full attention on her grama.

CHAPTER FOURTEEN

Destiny Allen was a very beautiful woman from Slovakia. Her large-framed, voluptuous body did not take away from her flawless skin, olive complexion, her large, clear blue eyes, her kind and generous mothering manner, or her way of making you feel totally at ease.

At 5'7", she didn't stand tall, but her presence was enormous. Her Slavic accent was subtle, but certainly there.

After the introductions, Melissa was asked to sit in the next room until she was called forward. Abby was asked to go with Destiny. At that moment, Destiny did not feel or know about Brenner. He decided to be with Abby, but kept his distance just in case he was found out by the famous Destiny Allen.

After the door was closed, Destiny held Abby's hand in both of hers and Abby instantly felt a warm rush of energy throughout her entire body. They released their hold and the rush was then gone.

"I wanted to get a reading on you before we begin", she announced while making a sweeping movement with her hand.

Destiny motioned for Abby to have a seat on the overstuffed couch in her office, while she sat in an off-white recliner across from her client.

Destiny waited and watched as Abby's eyes scanned the room.

Abby was quite impressed by what she saw. The pictures on the walls reminded Abby of gypsies with the scarf on the head but tied behind the neck, the long curly hair, the large hoop earrings, and the colorful material of their clothing.

There were other things like a palmistry pottery hand sitting on a side table, a very old and heavy book of spells on the floor by her desk, strands of beads and plain gold necklaces hanging from nails off the wall by the door, and a large box of incense on the corner of her desk.

Destiny saw Abby looking at the incense. "Incense is like radar for the spirit world. It helps them find their way to the person asking for their presence."

Abby's forehead wrinkled and she became embarrassed. "You could read thoughts?"

"I can", she laughed. "Keep looking around the room while I get myself ready."

Abby kept her thoughts at bay while she continued looking. She noticed that the furniture was mismatched but very functional and comfortable. The aura in the room was somewhat the same as in Abby's own living room.

Destiny was patient by letting Abby take her time and absorb everything around her, but now it was time to get down to business. "Please tell me what it is you seek from me?

"I met a man, uh, a ghost, and we want to be together." It sounded silly springing from her lips like that, but what else could she say under the circumstances. What she said was the truth.

Destiny did not skip a beat. She had heard all sorts of things in her long life and nothing made her heart skip a beat.

Abby looked down at her hands, which were fidgeting in

her lap. She wasn't sure if Destiny was going to take her serious, until she spoke again.

"So, if I could make this happen, how long would you like to be together?"

Abby was dumbfounded. Destiny didn't kid her, make fun of her, or think she was ridiculous. She was actually asking Abby how long she wanted to be together with Brenner.

Abby's mind was reeling and she jumped at a number. "Is two hours okay?" She made a face as if the woman across from her was going to yell.

"Two hours is enough time to do what you want to accomplish?" she asked looking straight into Abby's face. She watched her client nod and then asked Abby if she knew how the payment part worked.

Abby shook her head no. She was confused. What could this woman want for payment other than money being exchanged, she wondered.

Destiny smiled and explained the procedure just in case it was not clear.

"I can grant you anything you want, but there is a cost", she began. Destiny brought both hands up in front of her and touched all finger tips together like a web. "I will give you two hours with the man you love, and you give me one year of your life." She waited for Abby's reaction to the deal.

Abby was beside herself. Can this really be happening? Abby was awestruck. She sat closer to the edge of her seat and wanted it explained further. Before she had a chance to ask, Destiny brought it more to light.

"Abby, I am 193 years old."

Abby almost choked with doubt but continued listening to the older woman who held her fascination.

"I have granted wishes to many people in this world and all I ask is my normal payment of $50, plus one year of your life. Once you pay the small amount of money that is required, you sit back and wait for the spell of removing that one year, to be cast. This takes but a minute and then everything is done. Your wish is granted and we all get what we want. In the end, everyone is happy."

Abby couldn't believe it. She realized that she could have whatever she wanted and all she had to do was give up one year of her life. That seemed like such a small price to pay for happiness. "I agree", she answered whole-heartedly without any hesitation.

Destiny nodded, knowing that Abby fully understood what she was giving up. "Fine. Let us begin."

Abby was given the standard 'don't talk unless I ask you to' speech. And when Destiny asked her a question and it was her turn to answer, the answer must be short – a yes or no will do.

With the business part out of the way, they got down to the nitty-gritty and Destiny wanted more information. "I need you to sit still and open your mind. I want to read your thoughts."

Abby closed her eyes, which she thought would help, but her mind kept saying Brenner over and over again. She began contemplating what it would be like to really be with him, human-to-human. She couldn't help it. She was now obsessed with him and she knew it.

Destiny could see all the details that led up to Abby coming to this room today. She could see Brenner's name and face all over Abby's mind and she knew that they really did love each other.

When things got too quiet, Abby got curious. She opened one eye and watched as Destiny went into some kind of trance. She was certainly very much in the room, but part of her was not.

The aura of the room suddenly took on a new dimension. Abby found it odd that the strangeness she feels in the farmhouse, seemed to appear in that very room with them as well.

"Wait", Destiny began. "I feel someone in the room with us. Someone who wants us to know that he's here."

Abby's eyes widened and her ears had now perked up. She wasn't sure if she should speak, so she kept quiet and still.

Destiny's hands were now in the air, swirling and circling as if she was casting some kind of spell. "Appear before us in your state or another form, so we can know you are here. Come and state your feelings with the young lady seated across from me. We challenge your knowledge and welcome your ideas. Let us help you in whatever way we can."

Abby sat still while her eyes circled around the room. She was scared, but excited at the same time. Could this be real? Could Brenner really become alive again?

"Come to us, Brenner Jaxon", called Destiny. "Come and show yourself to me."

The magic was so strong that Brenner had no choice but to appear before Destiny.

There was a powerful pull from her world to his. It was untamed and demanding, thoughtful and kind, compelling and forceful. Brenner was lifted from his position behind Abby, and now was standing directly in front of Destiny.

Destiny's eyes were closed and her thoughts were strong. She focused on Brenner and Brenner alone. She dug into his soul and tried to suck out every bit of information that she could.

"I'm here", his mind telepathed to hers.

Destiny heard his soothing voice inside of her mind and a smile grew across her entire face. She felt her body relax as she made the connection with her intended soul. "Now we shall begin", she said smiling.

Abby was wondering what was happening. She watched Destiny smile and then the woman was quiet and seemed more at peace. Abby could see the frown lines and the smiles that the woman displayed, but didn't know why.

No one spoke for the next ten minutes or so and it became uncomfortable. Destiny was in her own world, communicating with Brenner, while Abby sat still and waited for her next instruction.

Brenner was surprised to find that Destiny was able to communicate with his subconscious soul, as if him and her belonged in the same body. When all this talk about him becoming alive began, he had his doubts. Now, he actually had hope that what they had all planned to do, would somehow work.

Destiny could feel his presence instantly, as well as his emotional pain. His thoughts were strong but wounded, and she was able to read exactly why he was still here and why he had not taken the next step to heaven.

Brenner, 35-years old and standing almost 6' tall, was in love with a simple woman of 23. His family had money, while her's did not. He was a decent Catholic boy, while she was a peasant.

Brenner fell in love with Hilary the moment he saw her. Her slender, but well-built body, captured his heart. Her smile melted his soul, and her voice has stayed in his mind to this very day. His parents knew of the silly infatuation and threatened to disown him if he did not do as he was told – leave her alone and marry the girl whom they will choose for him.

Brenner voiced his opinion and was forcibly locked away upstairs in his bedroom. He hated being locked up, but was ushered there with promises of a beating if he did not comply.

Unbeknownst to Brenner, his parents went to Hilary's home and brought with them a suitable man for her to marry, plus a handful of money with the promise that she move away and never contact their son again.

The girl's father ordered her to take the generous offers and they were wed that very night. The newly, married couple left right away and were never heard from again.

Brenner heard his parent's carriage driver start the horses just before 9pm. He summoned for the maid and inquired where his parents were going. The maid, thinking that she was doing the right thing, told Brenner of his parents plans. She told him this with hopes that it would settle him down.

It did not. He became even more agitated and shouted at her to get out. The news made him twice as determined to escape his confines.

Brenner desperately needed to get to Hilary before she left town with another man. Unrelentlessly he tried to escape but found that there was no way out.

Once he heard that they were home again, Brenner called for his parents to come to his room where he asked them of their whereabouts. They showed their presence in due time and his mother revealed where they had gone.

Brenner became angry with his mother. He turned to his father and waited for his words. None came. He turned back to Lillianna and threatened to kill himself if he was not allowed to marry who he wanted.

Lillianna laughed at her son for being so dramatic, then, failing to see that he might carry his threat out, taunted him to 'go ahead'. She informed her son that they had watched the girl get married and leave town with her husband. "There is nothing you could do other than to marry the girl which we have chosen for you."

Brenner had never been that angry. "I will not!" he ordered.

Brenner was beside himself with grief. The girl that his parents had chosen for him would greatly benefit both families' lives and he knew this. They would combine their wealth and then own half the county.

Brenner remembered the girl's appearance from their one and only meeting; small-boned, homely, well-dressed but only mildly pretty. Her spirit had been broken and she had her head lowered most of the time. He knew that this woman could never make him happy.

Lillianna felt that she knew her son well enough to know that he would be angry for tonight, but would be much better come the morning. She bid him good-night and then locked his door.

Brenner had never felt this kind of hurt or betrayal before. He couldn't believe that his mother could do this to him. He then hated his father for not stepping up, for not speaking his mind.

Brenner's tears rushed forth and his head started cramping. He needed to end his emotional hurt and bring pain to the persons responsible for tonight's horror. He knew just what he needed to do.

The next morning, when the maid came up to clean the room and bring him his breakfast, she found Brenner hanging from the rafters. The note beside his body read, "I died from a broken heart."

Destiny gulped out loud when she saw the vision of him hanging himself. She quickly opened her eyes to stop the next vision. Now she understood everything.

Brenner wanted to make sure that the clairvoyant knew that the past was now behind him. He regrets his decision and would very much like a second chance.

Brenner went on to show Destiny a picture from his mind – a picture of him smiling lovingly in Abby's direction, to show Destiny that this is the woman he now loves and wants to be with.

Destiny shed a tear as she felt all of his emotions and reasonings. She opened her eyes and looked towards a very sad and worried Abby. She now knew that the two lovers should be together. "Of course I will do everything in my power to help you." She stood up and hugged Abby real tight.

Melissa was called from the next room and the group sat and talked about what the next step would be. Destiny shared a bit of information about Brenner with the two ladies, but felt that the rest should be disclosed by Brenner himself.

"Can you give me a day or two to pull this off?" she asked to Melissa and Abby. "I need to make some phone calls, contact a few acquaintances, and get some more information on how to do this kind of spell."

Abby was intrigued.

Melissa was spellbound. "Is there anything that I can help you with?" her eyes were wide and her face close to Destiny's.

Destiny could definitely sense that Melissa had some powers, which could prove quite valuable down the line. Destiny made a mental note to sit with her after this spell was done. She believed that they would be spending a lot of time together in the future.

"Certainly, my dear. When the time is right, I will undoubtedly call upon you for help."

Melissa almost jumped out of her seat. With everything she had done in her life – spells, reading fortunes, reading people, etc… this will be the biggest thing that she was ever a part of. She wanted to scream for joy, but instead held her composure and thanked Destiny for her time and wisdom.

Destiny then turned to Abby and reached out for her hand. Taking it in between both of hers, she spoke. "I will call you once I know something. This *will* work, my dear. Of this, I am very sure."

"Thank you." Abby looked over Destiny's shoulder and into Brenner's happy eyes. She was pleased that he seemed just as thrilled.

Brenner couldn't wait to hold Abby in his arms, make love to her, and kiss her as he'd never done to anyone before.

Abby turned to Destiny. "Thank you for everything."

Brenner also looked over at Destiny. From mind-to-mind, he conveyed his thank you for all that she had done for them today. He could feel Destiny's welcome and smiled.

Abby, Melissa, and Brenner left and went straight to the farmhouse where they talked for another hour.

CHAPTER FIFTEEN

Destiny cancelled all her other plans and was busy placing calls to people whom she knew would be able to pull off this spell. She took a notepad and pen and jotted down names, their ages, and what they looked like.

Melissa — *28 years old and sister to Abby. No matter what, Melissa Hudson has to be involved. She had certain strong powers and would be able to help in a big way.*

Sylveeno — *currently has 119 years to live. He is from Russia. Looks good at 49 — his age when he was granted extra life. Hard, crusty face. Strong weathered hands, low eyebrows, stern expression, nice mouth, and very tall.*

Rosalynn Stefano has 141 years to live — comes from the high altitude area of Sicily. Her life when she was given extra years was 41. Very nice lady. — fussy about cleanliness and the way she dresses.

Dominic Majadori has raised 122 years — was born in Tuscany, Italy. Looks exactly like Enrique Iglesias, only a few years older. He was given his extra years at age 35. Proud of his heritage, strong and virile male, very tall and good looking, wonderful mouth and other facial features, strong hands and nicely kept. Chest like a god, simple waist and beautiful legs. Dresses immaculately, has fine taste in women and wine. His words carry a nice accent and seem to caress the air around him when he speaks.

Ariel Mathews — *a very proud-to-be-black woman now has 90 years and is from New Orleans. She was 44 when she was given extra years. The only black person in the world with this kind of power. Loud and strong voice, famous in her own right, knows her stuff when it comes to spirits and spells. Hair in tight curls like Shirley Temple. Dresses very well — jewelry on her fingers and bangles on her wrists. She is funny, and would fit in with everyone.*

Destiny looked at her list and agreed that this could definitely work. She was confident that these were the best people in the world to perform this spell.

Destiny made the calls to invite the list of people, and set a date. A week later, everyone arrived, introductions were made, and they were all told what they had been called for.

Destiny led the group as the meeting began. "You all have a vague idea about why you were summoned here today", she started. She waited and watched as they all agreed.

"In order to perform the chosen spell, we need to delegate who does what for the next meeting." Going around the room, Destiny asked all of the members what their strong suits are. This will help her to decide which avatar does what.

Ariel Mathews, with her strong personality, spoke up first. "I am great with mapping out the sky for horoscopes and life changes", she began. "I have some strange New Orlean powders and herbs that I use to perform love spells. In my hometown, I am most recognized with doing perfect match-making."

Rosalynn Stefano spoke up next. "I perform spells from the old country and use products that are not sold anywhere else in the world. I want to be the one who looks up the spell we use to implement the task of bringing these two people together. If I can't find it, I will consult with the elders back home."

Everyone quickly turned to the handsome man sitting next to Rosalynn. "Hi", he burst forth. "My name is Sylveeno and I was a mathematician in my younger days before I knew of my gift. I am confident that I am the best person to predict the longitude and the latitude to make the spell work its strongest magic. It must be done on the most perfect spot on the planet, and I know I can find it."

Destiny was getting excited at the prospect that this really could work. "My gift", she declared. "Is one of sight and in the foretold. I am a true clairvoyant. I talk to the dead and help with major decisions. I am affluent with magical power, and can and do perform readings where I can tell you about your future."

Dominic Majadori, a gorgeous man in any age or time zone, spoke next. "I dabble in black magic using the moon, its components, and all of its powers. I suggest that I know everything about this night orb, better than anyone else dead or alive."

Melissa was fascinated and just sat back in awe. She had practiced magic for years and thought that she had some real powers. Clearly, after tonight, she had nothing like what these people have sitting at the same table as her.

Once everyone got to speak and tell the others about their strengths, they talked about the kind of spell they thought might work in this instance. Of course, everyone had an opinion to share, and things eventually got worked out. The group talked for three hours and everyone was quite happy with the final outcome.

Destiny decided to end the meeting for the day. "Do we all know what jobs we need to do?"

The assembly nodded in agreement.

"Great", she laughed. Destiny clapped her hands together as a signal that the meeting was now adjourned. "See you all on Thursday." She stood up and watched as everyone slowly said their good-byes and headed for the door. She then made the room presentable while going over in her mind, all that was said during the meeting.

An hour later, Melissa caught up with Abby and they went for coffee. She told her sister everything that she saw and heard in the three hour meeting. "I'm still having trouble believing it even happened", she laughed.

Abby was still stunned that the whole thing could really work. She looked into her sister's eyes and tried to see the reality of the situation. Brenner died a long time ago. He was now a ghost. She wondered how he could be brought back to life again.

As if reading her thoughts, Melissa spoke up. "It's easy, really."

Abby's eyes went wide with surprise that Melissa got into her head. "Go on", she goaded.

Melissa put her cup down and started explaining. "Magic has no perfect answers. It is mostly made up of a strong belief, a great deal of wishing, true love, and ties directly with all the elements in the world."

Abby didn't know what to say. She looked into her coffee cup and mentally measured how much liquid was left to drink. She picked up the paper container and sipped the rest.

Melissa knew that Abby wasn't quite sure what to think about all of this, but hoped that her sister would place enough confidence in her to know that this could possibly, really work. "Trust me, okay?"

Without speaking another word, they finished their coffees and headed home.

Abby told Brenner everything that she learned from

Melissa about the meeting and the people who attended it. The happy couple was delighted but decided not to get their hopes up. They promised each other that they would keep themselves busy and wait to see what happened in the next meeting.

The group held another meeting a few days later. Everyone was asked to bring a magical scenario and a spell, and any other pertinent information they thought would help to make this work accordingly.

Destiny waited until everyone was seated before she began. She opened the meeting by clapping her hands together. "The meeting will now come to order!" She waited for everyone to stop talking and pay attention. "Who had the place?" she began.

"Everything points to Banff, Canada", Sylveeno stated as his hand went up in the air. He got his maps out and showed the group how he found the perfect spot to bring Brenner to life for two hours.

"See?" He pointed to the numbers as everyone around him rose from their chairs to get a better view. "51° 6' N & 114° 1' W makes this the perfect location." He went on to explain how he reached that conclusion.

Destiny looked around the room. "Does everyone agree?" She watched as they all nodded and smiled.

The spell was chosen by Rosalynn. Her hand went up as she recited the name of it. "The ingredients to perform the spell are a combination of both mine and Ariel's knowledge of herbs and scents."

Ariel smiled at her involvement.

"The spell that you chose is quite complicated", Dominic

piped up with his hand in the air. He was checking his personal book of spells before he said too much. "And it will only work as long as this spell is performed at precisely 11:10pm on Friday, October 31 of this year."

"Halloween?" someone stated from the corner of the room. "Isn't that a bit obvious?"

"But the moon and stars are perfect on that night", Ariel added. She put her notes on the tabletop for all who wanted to see. "The moon will be waxing and the stars will be in full bloom. This helps give more power to the spell."

"Also, it just so happens", Melissa giggled while becoming a bit embarrassed for speaking out of turn. "That it is on that very date, that the moon will enter a capital phase. What this means is that for a brief period of time, we will escape the maleficent influence and harmful magnetic radiation of this nocturnal celestial object..."

Abby piped in before Melissa had a chance to finish. "I thought everything always happened at midnight."

Ariel turned to her and rudely stated, "In this case, we can't wait until midnight." She turned to Dominic and continued. "He is right. The orb of influence is stronger at 11:10pm than it will be at midnight."

Abby became confused and interrupted again. "The orb of what?"

Rosalynn sighed, rolled her eyes, and then intervened. "As the planets move in their elongated orbits around the sun, they form various angular relationships with one another using the sun and the Earth as the centre. These are called aspects." She waited to see if Abby was truly listening.

Rosalynn was delighted when she saw not only Abby watching and listening, but a few of the others at the table were as well. She continued. "When these aspects are exact, it gives the spell the greatest impact. Sometimes, the effort of most aspects can be felt for some time before and after the exact moment.....hence the time and the place.

"The Orb of Influence", Ariel continued. "Is the range within which an aspect is in operation."

Abby's turn to sigh. "Sounds like black magic and hocus pocus to me."

Destiny stood up and walked to Abby's chair. She put her hands firmly on the back of it and leaned down while she spoke. "What we do is more like wish craft. Black magic is more for educational purposes. Those who wish to practice black magic must understand the laws of the universe....what goes around, comes back around. If you send out evil, it will eventually come knocking back at your door."

Abby turned around in her seat and smiled apologetically to show Destiny and the others that she was not mocking them. She was totally interested in what was happening and very appreciative of all that they were doing. "I'm sorry. I'm new at this and just curious."

Destiny hoped that she was now okay with everything. "Do you have any more questions?"

Abby thought for a brief second and then replied. "I have one more question."

A small mutiny began but Destiny hushed the others to silence while raising her flat hand towards the group. Then she looked at Abby and asked her to continue.

I've heard of white magic", she said. "Where does that fit in?"

Destiny knew that Abby was trying to understand so she tried to be patient with her. She slowly walked back to her seat, telepathically letting the others know that they've spent enough time on this matter and that it was time to get down to the real business at hand.

Destiny answered Abby quickly. "White and grey magic turns to black sometimes. For example, let's say you do a spell to obtain money. A week later someone in your family dies and leaves exactly what you need. What started out to be white magic, was actually gray magic, which then turns to black magic all in one clean swoop."

Melissa piped in to finish the answer. "You see, gray magic can turn white or black. That is why you should always do a divination before the spell is actually performed."

"So you can find out the outcome of the spell before it gets completed", said Sylveeno from across the room.

Melissa smiled and nodded in his direction as a thank you for helping Abby to understand.

"Divination?" Abby was really lost now.

Melissa completed her answer. "A divination is like a practice run. It gives a person a clearer understanding or view of the choice they are about to make." Melissa turned to the rest of the room full of people as she continued. "I will be doing this myself the night before the spell is to be performed, to make sure that we have all our ducks in a row."

Satisfied that the group had answered all of Abby's questions, Destiny turned to Dominic. "So the actual spell will be performed in Banff, on Friday, October 31 at 11:10pm." She waited for his nod. "And to confirm, this is better than at midnight, right?"

Abby turned towards Dominic, as do a few of the others, and questioned in her mind the same thing. She watched as the very handsome man slowly leaned forward, bringing his hands onto the tabletop and intertwined his fingers as he spoke.

Destiny sighed as he lectured. She loved his accent but not the incredibly long words that he constantly uses.

Dominic scanned the faces of all who sat around him and started to communicate like a professor conducting a class. "Ladies and Sylveeno", he began with a very authoritative tone. "This is the most encapsulated moment, the most indrawn point, and the source of the vibration that starts a new cycle that sends out a pulse. A new beginning, if you will. A beginning built upon results of the previous cycle. It is an idea in its purest or most direct form."

Dominic paused for effect as he stood up and started walking around the room.

"It is clarity, but very pure and seminal. Above all, it is a new signal that is strong enough to overcome and rise above the past and assert itself. This is a vision point and the only time and date to make this happen."

Destiny was left breathless. That was terrific, she admitted to her inner self. He was so eloquent in his delivery and manner that she wanted to fall in love with him, but knew it wouldn't work.

Dominic had been married seven times; none of his marriages made it past three years as his work always came first.

Rosalynn turned to Ariel and made the next statement. "I agree. I also found out that on that very night, at that very time, a major magnetic eruption will occur on the sun. When, for the length of several minutes, the spell will have even more power."

You could hear people agreeing and nodding around the table without looking or listening.

Destiny looked around the room with both palms up. "I think we have our time and date then, right? Are we all in agreement?"

"Halloween at 11:10pm, it is!" Ariel shouted with her right fist high up in the air. The rest of the group concurred.

"The two lovers will stay at the Banff Springs Hotel, arriving the day that the spell is to be performed." Destiny was reading from her notes. "The divination will take place the night before, in a room that will be chosen after we arrive. The room must be 'felt and read' by Melissa for vibrations and stimulation. The covenant will then gather together and wait for the outcome. If everything works out, we will go ahead with our plans. If not, well, we will deal with that when and if it happens."

"The spell will be performed in the next evening, right?" Abby was getting excited as everything was falling into place.

"Yes, my child." Rosalynn smiled and tapped Abby's hand lightly to reassure her.

Abby looked over her shoulder at Brenner and was pleased that he looked just as happy as she was with everything that was going on. She smiled and he smiled back.

"Meeting adjourned!" As everyone rose from their seats, Abby walked up to each and every one of the members of the covenant, and thanked them for their efforts and kindness.

Abby and Brenner then left the meeting feeling very blessed. They sat up and talked for hours about what they would want to have happen in those two hours where he becomes human.

The second week of October, Abby got a progress report from Destiny telling her that all was going well; that the plan was going ahead just as predicted.

Abby sighed at the good news. "Thank you very much for calling." Abby turned to Brenner and wished they could hug.

"Soon, my darling", he whispered as he read her thoughts. "Soon."

CHAPTER SIXTEEN

Casey Katan parked the car and looked in the rear-view mirror at his appearance. "Perfect, as usual", he commented to himself smugly. He played with his moussed, shoulder-length, wavy blonde hair to make it a bit more wild looking. He smoothed down both of his eye brows and flipped up his long lashes with a tongue-licked index finger. He blinked his icy-blue eyes and flashed his full lips to show a winning smile.

As he stepped out of the beat-up blue rental car, he popped a candy into his mouth to smell like menthol. He tugged at his light blue jeans, with slight tears at the knees and bum, and patted down his long-sleeved shirt. He fancied himself a cowboy without a ten gallon hat. He got more girls that way and the thought made him smile. Inside of his smug self he couldn't help but feel that Abby will want him back with no problem or hesitation. "No worries", he said to himself with confidence.

As each swaggered step clicked from boot hitting cement, memories came flooding back to Casey's mind. As his beautiful six foot frame walked closer and closer towards her new home, he remembered the last time that he saw Abigail Hudson.

They were in the front doorway of their home. As Abby bid him good-bye for the day, she had no idea that she would never see him again. It hurt him but he felt that it was for the best. "I'll call you tonight", he whispered as he lovingly kissed her cheek.

Unbeknownst to Abby, Casey had met someone at work and they had started an affair. They carried on their relationship for a few months before it turned serious. The next time he was told that he'd be going out of town for few days, the couple decided to make the trip longer; go away and explore a life together. Casey saw this business trip as the perfect opportunity to leave.

Instead of telling Abby that he had found someone new to be with, Casey decided to play this little romance thing through and see where it went. If it didn't last, he saw no need to tell Abby anything. If it was what he thought it would be, then he would end his romance with Abby and carry on with the new woman.

Casey left on his trip and things turned out great. He got caught up with his new lady love and their escapades together under the hot sun. He got his work done earlier than expected, and ended up with more downtime and fun. Things were more perfect than he could have expected and somehow he forgot all about his relationship with Abby and their life together.

Almost a week went by before he received a text message from a friend at work, asking him of his whereabouts. Casey called him and then learned of the plane crash. He was floored but decided that if people thought he was dead, he would play on that excuse and stay in hiding for a little while longer.

Casey swore his friend to secrecy and carried on with his new life.

Time was rushing by and everything was going great. Casey felt like he didn't want to ever end what was happening.

Surprisingly, Casey and his lady friend hit a snag in the road a little while ago and she left. Things came to a sudden halt and he saw no way out but to return to his old life.

Casey came back to town and tried to call Abby but she had moved and changed her phone number. Determined to win

Abby back, Casey hired a private investigator and within a few weeks he had everything he needed to contact his ex-girlfriend again.

Abby heard the knock and ran to the front entrance. "Coming!" she called. She opened the door and was shocked to see him. She took a step or two backwards, both hands covering her shocked expression, and then she ran into his arms screaming his name at the top of her lungs. "Ca-a-s-e-ey!"

Nick pulled up behind the faded blue wreck and realized that Abby must have company. He was stopping by for a surprise visit but hesitated when he saw Abby hugging a man who she was calling Casey.

Without turning off the motor, Nick slowly put the car into park and watched the two people laughing and embracing on the majestic front porch. He leaned forward in his seat, rolled down the passenger window, and listened to how happy Abby was that Casey was alive and apparently back in her life again.

"So, you do remember me then?" Casey laughed cautiously when they were face-to-face again for the first time in months. He wasn't sure what to expect.

"Of course I do", she gushed as she touched his hair, his face, and his shoulders. She kissed his mouth and cheeks over and over again. "I can't believe you're really here." Her mind was overloading with information but she didn't want it to stop. Casey was alive and back in her life and she couldn't be happier.

Casey was glad that the hard part was over. Now to reel her in.

"Oh my goodness!" she cried as she pushed their bodies apart. Everything about the memorial service and his apparent death came flooding into her mind.

"How did you get here? Where have you been?" She had a million more questions but Casey motioned that he wanted to come inside to talk and get reacquainted.

Nick's eyes and hand went to the large bouquet of multi-colored flowers that lay so delicately on the seat beside him. *When Abby hadn't called him, he decided to make another move by sweeping her off her feet and inviting her out to dinner.*

Nick felt his chest tighten and he wanted to throw up. He sat up straight in his seat, moved his hand from the flowers to his tie, and smoothed it down from top to bottom. Nick was hoping that he was also calming down his racing heart at the same time.

Nick took one more look towards the front porch and the woman that he fell in love with. It then took another second to sink in that what he could have had with Abby, was now over and done with.

Nick took a deep breath, put his newly-cleaned and washed vehicle into gear, and sped off as a giant tear slid silently from his right eye.

Brenner went to Abby's side when he heard the commotion outside, and the talking inside. He barely saw a car drive off, but then he turned and saw Abby hug this new man and this made him want to stay close by.

Brenner hid so he could hear and see everything. He listened closely as Casey described to Abby the details of what happened after he left her side.

Brenner watched as Abby listened and reached out to Casey several times, holding his hand in hers. Brenner watched as he saw a sly Casey pull Abby into his web of lies and deceit.

Casey told Abby about the plane crash and all he knew about the details. Of course, he lied through his teeth and configured the information to suit his own needs.

Once he was sure that Abby had believed him, Casey went on to explain how, once he was released from the hospital and remembered his name and address again, he tried to get hold of her. He said he'd been trying for the past month, since the beginning of September, to come back to her side. He then got worried because she had moved from their home and changed her phone number. *Abby disconnected her home phone and bought a cell phone for simplicity.*

Casey went on to explain how he asked everyone for a stick of information but chided that no-one would tell him where she had gone. Casey lowered his head and made himself look sad to get her sympathy vote.

After his huge sob story, Abby fell into Casey arms, completely forgetting about Brenner or their plans.

Brenner listened and watched from close by, but didn't let on that he was near. He could feel that she had forgotten about him and his heart was broken, but he didn't know what to do. His focus returned to Abby when he heard the sound of rap music being played in the room by the couch.

Casey's cell phone went off and he struggled to get it out of his pocket. Once he saw the display number, his expression went blank, his skin white. Casey stood up and said that he needed to answer the call right away. "Business. I'll be right back."

While Casey walked off, Abby relived the words that he said about how difficult it was finding her again. "How romantic", she swooned.

Brenner came out of hiding and stood beside Abby for a quick second. He wanted to be near her but didn't make himself known as something more pressing came up. Brenner turned and bee-lined for Casey when he heard the words, 'I Love You' coming from his mouth.

Casey had just been told that his girlfriend of the past few months had made a mistake and now she wants to have him back. She asked him where he was and he gave her the general area. He said that he needed a day or two to think about what she had just offered. At the end of their conversation, he said that he would call her back and then he hung up.

Casey returned inside to the living room where Abby was waiting, and asked for something to eat or drink. "Whatever you have on hand is fine."

Abby didn't hesitate. She was caught up in the moment and not thinking of anything or anyone else. She rushed off to make something for him, while Brenner stayed near Casey and watched his every move.

Casey, smug and full of himself, stood up and moved around the small room gently touching everything in his way. He recognized some things and saw other things that he assumed belonged to the previous owner.

Casey knew that his new girlfriend wanted to have him back again, but maybe being with Abby might be a better bet right now. He would take a moment to see which scenario would suit him better.

Abby brought the food and drink into the area where Casey was sitting and they talked for a while as Brenner listened from behind a wall. Another hour passed by before Casey asked for something more to drink. Abby got up to get it just as Brenner sensed something strange outside.

The girlfriend was arriving in a flurry of angry energy. She was only a few minutes away.

Brenner knew that he didn't have much time. He quickly followed Abby to the kitchen. He made himself known and tried not to scare her.

She hushed him from talking but Brenner needed Abby to know what was about to happen, so he continued.

Abby tried not to listen because she thought that Brenner was jealous. She was hoping that he would understand the situation and told him that she would speak with him later about it.

Brenner knew that his time was limited. He spoke quickly and was very convincing. He finally got all the words out and while Abby didn't want to, she finally believed him.

Casey, alone and bored in the living room, heard a car hurriedly pull up outside. He stood up and looked out the large front window. He gasped out loud when he saw Arleena rush out of the car and storm towards the house. He noticed her face and how angry she looked and did not want to face that problem in Abby's home.

Casey panicked and sat back down, trying to think about his next move.

Abby came back into the living room and immediately confronted Casey about the phone call and his girlfriend; her heart breaking with every second that passed. She watched closely as Casey hesitated and tried to think of one lie after another.

"What are you talking about?" he finally queried.

This caused Abby to become confused. Now it was her turn to lie. "I heard your conversation when you were on my porch, and now I want the truth."

Before he could answer, a strong knock banged against the front door. "Casey! I know you're in there!" a female yelled with extreme anger. "I'm sorry. I screwed up. I want you back. Please, let me in."

Everyone could hear that she sounded desperate as her pleading continued to get stronger.

Casey sat still with no emotion or expression. He pulled the glass of liquid close to his mouth and pretended that he didn't hear anything.

Brenner watched and felt sorry for Abby.

Abby stared at her estranged lover as he tried to hide from the woman outside. She was beginning to believe that the man before her had no sympathy or feelings. Is this the same man that I wanted to marry, she wondered. This cold-hearted, lying cheater?

Abby couldn't take it anymore. She felt sorry for the woman crying on her porch and banging against her solid door.

Abby stood up and ran to her front entrance. "Can I help you?" she demanded as the door swung open.

Arleena looked her up and down and then pushed past Abby and rushed into the livingroom to confront her boyfriend. "There you are!" she shouted wildly.

Casey wasn't sure what to do so he just sat there making one face after another like he didn't know who Arleena was or what she wanted with him. He was still not sure which girl to be with so he just sat back and watched as the situation played itself out.

"What do you have to say for yourself?" Arleena demanded. She stood with one long, tanned leg forward, her hands on her unshapely hips, and her gum being chewed in a rather loud and fierce manner.

Abby couldn't believe what she saw before her. Arleena was very tall and lean. She was probably in her early 20's and wearing hippy-style clothing. Her long unruly hair, hung down to her waist and looked like there was a weave or two attached somewhere inside.

Casey glanced in Abby's direction and waited for her to speak. Her saw the lost look on her face and didn't know what to say. "Abby?" he called trying to get her attention.

Abby's focus was totally enthralled on Arleena. She had no knowledge of anyone else in the room.

When Abby didn't respond, Casey felt that he had blown it and didn't have a chance with her anymore.

Casey, feeling like he had no other choice, stood up and passionately ran into Arleena's arms. "Thank you for coming back to me. I missed you so much."

Casey took Arleena in his arms and kissed her mouth like they were about to make love right there and then.

If he couldn't have Abby back, he would take the next best thing.

Abby watched and wanted to die. She believed him. She believed that Casey loved her and now she felt like a fool.

Much to Abby's surprise, Arleena turned around and thanked Abby for taking such good care of her fiancé for her. She stuck her hand out and introduced herself to Abby. "I'm Arleena."

Abby gasped in horror and felt her knees buckle beneath her. She didn't say a word but shook the girl's hand like a fish. She placed her other hand to her chest and flopped down on the chair behind her.

Brenner saw what was happening and sent out a ball of energy to Abby, which helped her with her thoughts and balance.

Casey, sensing that things will not work out with Abby after this, said his thank you's and good-byes. He put one hand against Arleena's back and pushed her forward. As he moved past Abby, he tried to kiss her on the cheek but she backed up, refusing to even make eye contact with him. He left her home snidely saying that it was her loss.

After the door closed, Abby turned and said sorry to Brenner. "Could you ever forgive me?"

Brenner smiled and his heart softened. "Without any hesitation or repercussion."

Brenner understood the situation between Abby and Casey and knew that she was fooled by him. He held no bad feelings towards her and was happy that the past has now been permanently put behind them.

Abby wanted so much to hold him and kiss him for his kindness. "Thank you, Brenner. I promise I will make this up to you."

"I know you will", he said smirking. He now felt that he had moved leaps and bounds closer to her heart.

Abby heard the two car motors start and then she surmised that Casey and Arleena had driven off together.

Abby sighed heavily and promised herself that she would never give Casey another thought again.

CHAPTER SEVENTEEN

On October 30, the day before the event, the members of the covenant gathered together in Banff to make sure that every detail was attended to and everything went according to plan. Each member was given a certain task to fulfill. Each member was told the rundown of things that would happen while they were there.

Destiny checked her watch. It was 9 am and the meeting was about to begin. "The covenant will now come to order." Destiny clapped her hands together to bring everyone's attention to the matter at hand.

Melissa sat next to Destiny as her right-hand person. *This seat was held for the second-in-command and holds high respect and utmost admiration from everyone in attendance. Melissa was very grateful when asked by Destiny to sit there.*

Melissa got very excited as she was handed the note that contained the ingredients and words to the spell. Destiny also formally bestowed upon her, the honor to oversee that all was done to perfection…an honor that Melissa will not soon forget.

The committee went over all the details for the next day's events, and then they broke up into smaller groups.

Destiny took a few members of the covenant to the place where the spell will be performed. Together they scouted the area, saw what had to be changed or moved, and counted out the steps to visualize where everyone should be standing during the ceremony.

A few of the members stood still or strolled around the spot with their arms spread open wide, palms up, eyes closed, and felt the aura within their bodies.

When everyone was happy and content with the spot that had been chosen and the energy that it gave off, they started talking about how to set things up to prepare for the 'Moment of Change'. An hour later, they bid their good-bye's and confirmed to meet the next day.

Melissa, in the meanwhile, took a few soothsayers with her as she scouted the many rooms of the hotel for the perfect place to hold the divination. It took her almost half an hour, but once she found the perfect room, she began her preparations.

Sylveeno dropped the bag with all the items necessary for the divination, and started pulling things out.

Rosalyn drew the curtains as Melissa pulled a large square table into the middle of the room. She slowly sat down and put her feet flat on the floor, leaving a 12-inch space between them. Melissa lit the candle in the middle of the table while waving her hands to move the smoke towards her face. She then closed her eyes and hummed a solemn song in a chanting manner while swaying side-to-side.

Ninety seconds later, Melissa encouraged everyone to gather close and watch as she pulled out a package of tarot cards from the front pocket of her large hand-knitted sweater. Sylveeno dimmed the lights as Melissa slowly laid one card down on the table at a time. She whispered the meaning of each card and detailed how it will affect the spell.

Sylveeno had never been to a divination before and was completely entranced by the event, and the person conducting it.

No one else in the room spoke. The room was in almost

total silence as, one-by-one, the cards revealed the mystical outcome of the powerful spell.

The divination took almost an hour and Melissa was very pleased with the conclusion. The lights came back on, the curtains opened, and everyone could talk again. Melissa hugged everyone in attendance for a job well-done. She encouraged them to all have a good sleep until they met again the next day.

Destiny and Melissa met up with one other in the front lobby ten minutes later to discuss all the new and remaining details. After their 22-minute meeting, being quite satisfied that everything was now going to be perfect, they embraced and said good-night.

Before going to bed, Melissa called Abby and told her all of the exciting news that had taken place since she had arrived in Banff.

Abby was not only overjoyed at what was happening, but very proud of her dear sister. She suddenly realized that everything that Melissa had done in her life up until now, brought her to this point.

The girls talked for a few more minutes before saying good-night.

Abby and Brenner arrived at the Banff Springs Hotel at 11:30am on October 31. Abby got the key to their accommodation and together they found their way.

Abby placed her bags on the floor and scanned the entire room. "I love it", she said quietly. "I love everything about this room." She turned to look at Brenner's face and smiled when she saw that he was just as pleased.

Abby reached into the larger of the two bags and pulled

out a few items. The candles were seductively placed around the 12'x16' area, and then she laid her skimpy outfit flirtatiously on the bed as Brenner watched.

Brenner encouraged her with an eager eye. He couldn't wait until that night and wished for the time to go faster.

Brenner was enthralled as Abby took her perfume and sprayed the bed, as well as the air above it. He saw how much pride she was taking in preparing the room for the night's event, and he blessed her for it.

With everything as it should be in their room, Abby and Brenner went downstairs and met with the covenant one more time before the spell got performed. They were very excited and looking forward to later on in the evening.

The members of the covenant were told to gather at noon in the large meeting room by the check-in desk. Abby and Brenner arrived last, but seconds before Destiny had started the meeting.

"The meeting will now come to order", she demanded as she clapped her hands together. "Welcome, and let us begin."

Everyone listened closely to the results of the divination, and the feelings about the spot that had been picked to perform the spell.

Happy that the divination went well, Abby was more encouraged than ever that this will work.

The group talked for another hour about this and that, and then dispersed until later. Some went for a walk, some explored the immediate area, some relaxed and did nothing, and some paced the floor from nerves.

The time seemed to pass slowly as the group waited for the perfect hour.

By 10pm, the energy of the crowd geared up. The table outside needed to be set up, ingredients had to be checked one last time, the sky desired to be checked for perfection, and the group was required to get dressed in their formal spell clothing. *The outfits include long flowing, sometimes flowery dresses for the girls, and loose, black clothing for the men – shoes were optional.*

As the time approached, everyone seemed ready and headed out to the appropriate spot. Twenty small candles were placed a foot apart in a large circle, and lit up as everyone gathered together. Everyone and everything pertaining to tonight, was placed inside the glowing ring.

As she stood in the field near the big hotel, Melissa felt great pride as she held a long piece of paper in her hand. She still couldn't believe that she got chosen to lead the group in this spell. Her heart was beating strong, the goose bumps on her skin were intensified by the cool air, and the prospect that this might actually work made her happier than she had ever been in her life.

Melissa took a quite moment to herself and looked towards the heavens. She sent out a special blessing and a kiss to her young daughter, Echo, who should be fast asleep at her best friend's home.

Echo felt her mother's thoughts and smiled to herself. "Good luck", she whispered via mental telepathy to her mother.

Melissa gushed with love and then came back to her immediate reality. She gathered her strength as she looked around at all the people in the semi-circle and smiled.

"Are we ready?" she asked with a great deal of enthusiasm. She checked her watch for the correct time.

The group nodded and joined hands as the cold air seeped into the pores of their bodies. Brenner stood behind Abby and watched in wonder.

At precisely 11:05pm, Melissa commenced. "Let us begin", she announced.

Melissa looked down at all the ingredients listed on the paper and asked Destiny to come forward. Everyone watched as she walked over to the large table.

"One pink rose", she began. Destiny lifted the items one-by-one, showing them to everyone in the covenant, as well as to the moon and the stars above. "We have some ground vanilla pods, a dried avocado, one red candle and one violet candle - both inscribed with a love Rune. Some ginger, jasmine oil, a few drops of Abby's blood, a red cloth, and a sheet of red paper."

Once the items were presented to the group and the sky, everything was put back down on the table and Destiny took a step back.

Everyone now watched as Rosalynn took a step forward. She stood in front of the large bowl sitting on the table and waited for her instructions.

Ariel left the semi-circle by taking a few steps towards the table and lit the two candles. At exactly 11:10pm, she raised her hands in the direction of the sky and started delivering the spell towards the heavens. Everyone smiled and held hands as she began.

"By the light of the candles and the moon", she shouted with great joy. "Grind up the avocado with the vanilla pods and the ginger. When it is a fine powder, add 5 drops of Abby's blood. But as you expel each drop into the mixture, we shall all say the following words together:

All the members in the covenant could see and feel the changes happening almost immediately.

"Spirit of the South." The entire group turned and faced the south. "Ancient one of fire and passion. With this drop of blood I call upon you to bring the lovers together."

The white clouds against the dark sky started moving and changing shape.

"Spirit of the West." The group turned and faced the west. "Ancient one of water and peace. With this drop of blood I call upon you to bring the lovers together."

The winds changed direction and the air now became loud and musty.

"Spirit of the North." The group turned and faced the north. "Ancient one of earth and fertility. With this drop of blood I call upon you to bring the lovers together."

Below their feet, the earth gave its blessing for the happy union by moving and rumbling.

"Spirit of the East." The group turned and they all face east. "Ancient one of air and strength. With this drop of blood I call upon you to bring the lovers together."

Ariel lowered her hands and looked directly at Abby's face. With the cold air swirling around them, starting to blow and make noise, and the clouds above starting to gather into strange forms, Abby knew that she must now make her speech to the elements.

With everyone back in line, the group formed a semi-circle and all held hands as Abby stood in front of the covenant with her back towards the table. She raised her face and closed her eyes and let the full moon shine down on her skin. She waited until the air around her gave its permission to begin. She then opened her eyes and moved her hands out and to the sides, away from her body. In a booming voice, she delivered these words from her heart.

"Akasha!" she shouted as tears of joy started cascading from her eyes. "The spirit element of all things on Earth." Abby held up the last drop of blood in the vial and showed it to the sky. The moment was more powerful than even she thought it would be.

"With this drop of blood, I call upon you to combine the powers called forth, and bind my lover's spirit to mine so that we can be together."

The sky suddenly lit up with a terrific thunder bolt, giving a crashing sound like that of two freight trains slamming into each other at high speed.

Everyone was shocked at the loudness but remained steadfast in their spot while Abby walked back to the semi-circle.

Melissa stepped forward again to conduct the rest of the spell. She waited until Abby made her way back into her place in line, and Rosalynn then made her way back to the table. Melissa lifted her hands and began speaking in a strong, loud voice.

"Using the new paste, draw the love Rune, 3 times, on the piece of red paper and empower it. Wait for it to dry and then fold the paper in half."

Everyone watched as Rosalynn fanned the paste to dry it quickly. Once the paper had been folded, Melissa continued.

"Now, take the rose and smear it on any remaining paste." Everyone watched.

"Place the rose in the red cloth and anoint it with Jasmine oil." Melissa waited for this to happen.

"Now, using the red candle, set fire to it and put it in a bowl until the flame has gone out." Again, everyone watched the very bright display. Two minutes later, Rosalynn blew the last of the small fire out.

"Grind up any lumps left in the ash or remove any stubborn bits, then put the ash into the folded paper and put it in an envelope. Seal the envelope with a blob of wax from the candle and present it to Abby."

Everyone watched as this was done. Abby reached out to accept the envelope and bowed to thank her. Abby turned to show Brenner and he also bowed his appreciation.

Melissa continued. "The spell has now been completed."

Immediately, all the elements have calmed down and the world seemed to have changed somehow.

The members of the covenant exhaled with relief and joy as they congratulated each other on a job well-done. One-by-one, the members of the group went from being very serious, to relaxed and quite happy. The spell had been performed. Now, all they had to do was wait.

Sylveeno rushed to Melissa's side and congratulated her on a job well-done. He was very proud of her and would've liked the chance to know her better, but he was only in town for this one spell. Maybe on his next trip.

The lovers were instructed to go to their hotel room and prepare for what comes next.

The happy couple bid everyone a huge thank-you, and off they went.

CHAPTER EIGHTEEN

Abby got into her shear nightie and stood in the middle of their luxurious room. Brenner suddenly appeared before her. They both knew that if everything went well, the effects of the spell should start happening in the next sixty seconds.

The couple stood three feet apart with candles of every color and size, lit and burning all around the room, throwing shadows on every wall and piece of furniture. Soft music was playing off in the distance while they waited for the moment when they could be together.

Two strong people unpredictably become shy and frozen in their tracks. Last minute nervousness became the theme of the final few seconds.

All of a sudden, a strange odor came creeping into the room. With it came a soft, eerie breeze – strong enough to move a few hairs out of place, but not strong enough to move a cotton dress. A small rumbling started under their feet and they were not sure what was happening. The whole room gradually took on a different feel; strange yet comforting.

Without moving her head, Abby noticed the clock. It was time. She turned back to Brenner, locked eyes and waited.

Brenner began to feel different, whole as if his skin was suddenly becoming alive again. He looked down and saw his hands, solid for the first time in years and it made him smile. His head became dizzy and his body wavered as power came to legs that were not used to supporting weight.

Abby watched as each part of Brenner came clearer and

clearer into view. It was as if he had been so far away and was now becoming closer.

The outline of his face and body was becoming more defined and she was pleasantly surprised at how beautiful he truly was. Abby was so happy that she wanted to cry and laugh at the same time, but held it in for the moment.

As Brenner became real, he took a breath and could feel the air go inside of his lungs. It hurt at first, but was exhilarating at the same time. He laughed out loud at the wonderful gift that he was being given.

Brenner wiggled his fingers and toes and moved his mouth as he tried to speak out loud. Before a single word uttered from his beautifully shaped lips, he took a step closer to Abby and looked into her perfect eyes. "I've waited for this moment for more than a lifetime", he said poetically.

A tear fell from her eye as she listened. Her body started trembling with anticipation and happiness. The moment was so surreal and she wondered if she was dreaming.

"Please know that whatever happens here tonight, you could never disappoint me", he whispered.

Abby blushed. She wasn't sure what to do next but knew that their time was extremely limited. She took a step closer to him and reached out her hand to caress his face. "And you could never disappoint me either."

She gently touched the left side of his forehead, his eyebrow, his cheek, and his entire mouth with her thumb. She could feel every line, every new whisker, and every small indent in his skin.

Brenner wanted to cry. Her touch was more than heavenly. He tried to watch her expression as she continued stroking and touching his skin, but he couldn't help but close his eyes to stop his own tears from pouring out. Her movements were wonderful and ever so sensuous. He could barely feel her skin touch his, but it made him quiver all over.

Abby went on tip-toes and kissed his lips with her own. It was quick, gentle, and soft.

Brenner didn't know it could feel that good. His eyes opened quickly at the same moment his mouth got covered with Abby's slightly parted lips.

Her lips were moist, soft, and very eager to kiss all night. He had not been kissed in many years and loved the feeling that went all over his body from the alluring touch.

Their kisses started slowly, teasing and dancing by moving their heads this way and that. A minute later, their movements became stronger and his lips wanted more.

Brenner reached his arms tenderly around her back and slowly pulled her even closer to him. His breath quickened and his heart raced the more the space between them lessoned. The kissing was now becoming aggressive and both knew it wouldn't be long before they would each want more.

Brenner died a virgin and lived alone for too many years. This was to be the very first time that he'd ever been with a woman in his life. He was sure that he'd know what to do and how when the time came, but he wasn't sure of how he should proceed at the moment.

Abby could feel his manhood pressing into her leg. She

knew it wouldn't take long before they were undressed and making love.

They kissed a few more times and then took a step apart while holding each other's hands. Abby smiled as she reveled in how soft his skin was. His thin, long fingers begged for her attention as they intertwined with hers.

With their eyes locked on one another, Brenner took a step closer and then kissed her neck. She smelled wonderful. He kissed her shoulders and he could feel her moan as she turned her head to give him better access. This made him want her even more.

The turmoil between the internal sex and the external needing to be together as quickly as possible, was more than either of them could handle. Both people knew that they must to go slowly and savor every second, every bit of contact, but it was getting harder to control.

Abby delighted in his touch, his smile, and his caresses. She moaned to herself when she saw Brenner look deeply into her eyes as he tried to guess what she was thinking. Abby kissed him again and begged him to take her.

Brenner, not being able to hold out much longer, moved her towards the bed and laid her down, holding the back of her head with a strong hand. When her head met the pillow, he rose his body slightly and took in the beauty that was to be his for the asking. He looked at her shape up and down and loved every inch of what he saw beneath him. He knew he couldn't wait much longer. She had to be his, and now, or he would bust.

Abby loved how Brenner looked at her. He seemed to drink in her thoughts and her emotions, as well as her newly-tanned body. She was enchanted when he studied her as if he was never going to see her again and wanted to make a memory of the moment. She could feel his eyes roam across her body, as if they were touching every hair and molecule.

Abby wanted him now more than ever. She moved her hands up behind his head. She pulled him down closer and parted her lips.

Brenner looked down at her expression and saw her face approaching his own. He saw her open lips and he couldn't resist. He raced to meet them while falling flat against her chest. He had forgotten what a woman smelled like, and how she moved and felt. He had forgotten the curves and softness of a woman's body. He had kissed many, but never went further…..until tonight.

Abby wanted to slip into a delightful coma when his full lips touched hers. Her hands roamed all throughout his beautiful dark hair, as his hands roamed all over the skin beneath him that was exposed to the air.

Many tears slipped from Abby's eyes as her mind had trouble believing that this was all happening, and that it was real. His touch, his smell, and his manhood, were all too good to be true.

Brenner lifted his body slightly, and without speaking, asked for his lover's permission to remove her one and only piece of clothing.

Abby happily nodded a firm yes.

Brenner smiled as her eyes gave their happy consent. He then unhurriedly took off her silky nightie.

Abby had nothing on underneath, but was not embarrassed.

She watched as he unhurriedly viewed all that was on display.

Brenner was beside himself in wonder. Abby had a perfect body – toned, tanned, and beautifully proportioned. He looked back into her striking eyes and slowly brought his hands up to the sides of her face. He gently grabbed her head as he said, "Thank you" into her mouth over and over again between kisses.

Abby enjoyed the kisses but knew that their time was running out. She pushed him up and away from her body. He was now standing beside the bed when she removed the little bit of clothing that he had on. She was pleased when he obliged without a fight.

Now it was Abby's turn to view what was on display. The well-toned body of Brenner left nothing to the imagination. He was also very perfectly proportioned, in every way possible.

Abby chuckled as Brenner put both hands up in the air and twirled twice for her. "See anything you like?" he joked.

Abby grabbed his right hand as she lay back down on the bed and coaxed him to follow.

As Brenner's naked body came onto the bed again, he spread Abby's legs and found his new home. He looked and touched everything lightly as she moaned and struggled to keep her mind and soul together.

Brenner got closer and with his hands, he touched her moist treasure but didn't linger. With his mouth, he kissed the skin of her legs from her toes to her thigh. With his breath, he teased her from one hip bone to the other, stopping in the middle an extra second or two for effect.

A tormented Abby lay struggling. She wanted to grab him and make him get on top. She wanted him more than she had ever wanted any man in her whole life. Her body was on fire, it was wet and swollen, and it was terribly turned on. She knew in her mind that he needed a few minutes to adjust, but her body had other thoughts.

Brenner loved how she moved and twisted beneath his hands and mouth. He very much enjoyed how she moaned and groaned. Watching her move beneath him, he knew that he would not be able to wait too much longer before he would need to enter her.

Brenner placed his body so that her legs were now outside of his own. His chest was on top of hers and they were both sweating from the anticipation and excitement of the moment. They locked eyes and knew that it was time.

Abby spread her legs and raised her knees to give him better access.

Brenner felt her move and looked down. He positioned himself at the wet and inviting opening with his hand, and the tip of his penis went inside. He moaned at the incredible feeling of entry.

Abby's head went back with a great deal of force as she stifled a scream. It felt more marvelous than she could have imagined.

Brenner's eyes closed and his mind exploded at how warm and wet she was. He pushed a little more and wanted to melt at how delicious she felt. He opened his eyes for a quick second to see Abby's face. Content that she was okay, he continued.

Abby wanted to cry out loud for happiness and joy. Her whole body was consumed with wonderful sensations that had never happened before. Her hair, her skin, her toes all felt these feelings. Her head whipped backwards again as a small sound leaped from her throat. She then felt him inch another part of himself inside her tight opening.

The sensations were too much for him. Every cell, every nerve ending, every drop of liquid that escaped his body, gave him a thrill to last forever.

Suddenly, everything about where they were, disappeared. Everything about time was erased from the world. Two people together as one – one almost thirty years old, and the other, it's hard to know.

Brenner couldn't help but thrust more steadily the further he got inside. He was hard and throbbing, shaking uncontrollably, and all because he was having trouble going leisurely. Abby was so warm and wet and it was driving him crazy. She was tight and he felt everything around himself.

He thought his head would burst with the wonderful feelings that ran throughout his body and soul. Every small push was a new sensation, every inch created another orgasm.

Brenner was now all the way in.

Abby could feel his entire length inside of her. He was wonderfully built and she moved with him in perfect rhythm.

Brenner moved his right hand under her body, to the

lower part of Abby's back, while his mouth covered her neck and face with kisses.

She had her hands on his back, feeling every inch of his skin, and holding onto him as if he had wanted to leave her bed.

Abby felt him grow harder inside of her while he slid quickly in and out. She held onto his strong shoulders and taut muscles as he now pounded against her with all of his might. She felt his breathing – labored and strong. She heard deep noises like that of a growl from a wild animal, come from his throat.

Abby loved everything about this moment. She felt herself sink into yet another orgasm as she gasped for air. She saw the stars go off behind her eyes and brought a hand up to the top of her head for fear that it would come off from the power.

The orgasm seemed to go on forever, or maybe there was just more than one happening. Abby could hear herself screaming while she tried to keep the feelings going.

Brenner also screamed, and then fell into the crook between Abby's neck and her shoulder. His breathing was hard and it came in short spurts. It seemed as if he couldn't and wouldn't be able to catch his breath again, but he soon recovered. When he did, he looked into his lover's beautiful face below him and used his hands to wipe away the hair and sweat from her cheeks and forehead. He then kissed every part of her head while they remained joined as one.

"Are you alright?" he asked softly. He really wanted to know.

Abby giggled. "I'm deliciously wonderful." She reached her lips up to his and kissed him soft and long. "Thank you for tonight", she whispered as she lay her head back down. She gazed into his beautiful eyes as she waited for him to respond.

Brenner again moved his hands to caress everything on her face. "The pleasure was most certainly mine", he began. "It is I who should be thanking you, and I do, most definitely thank you."

The bell went off on the side table which brought them both back to reality. That strange smell was again part of the room and with it came the slight breeze. When the aura of the room started changing, Abby locked eyes with Brenner and held on. They both knew that their time was up, but both wanted it to continue.

Abby saw the tears forming in Brenner's eyes and she screamed. "No-o-o-o-o-o!"

Brenner seemed to slowly melt away as she held him as tight as she could. Abby embraced him as long as she was able to, but soon there was nothing but air.

Abby threw herself from the bed and crumbled onto the floor. She could still feel the tears that he left behind, against her cheeks. They were mixing with her own new set that now sprang from her eyes.

Abby felt the last kiss that he placed on her forehead as he said good-bye, and it nearly killed her. "I don't want you to go!" she wailed into the air.

"I will always be here with you", he stated as if from afar. "No matter what."

Abby looked up towards the voice and saw Brenner as he was before. He was a ghost again and close by her body.

She knew in her mind that this was the plan before they even got started tonight. Abby had to think about it and then decided that the situation while not perfect, will do until they could figure out another way.

Abby moved towards him and got as close as possible. "Promise me that you will never leave me." She glanced into his eyes as he looked down into hers.

"I promise, my love." It broke his heart not to be able to reach out and wrap her in his embrace, but he knew the deal.

Abby reluctantly turned and covered her body with the sheet from the nearby bed. She was not embarrassed, but merely a bit cold. She walked towards him again and tried to touch him. She was not surprised to find that there was nothing but air. She walked back to the bed and sat down, her back towards him.

Brenner could feel her pain but knew that this was only planned for two hours. He hated the thought that he could never touch her again, or feel her breath against his body, but a deal was a deal. Two hours was all that they could have. Two hours was all that they had asked for.

One hundred and twenty minutes together with Abby, flesh-to-flesh, was what Brenner would always be grateful for.

"My love", he began. "I will always be here with you. You will never be alone again."

Abby's tear-stained face looked towards Brenner and she started to cry again. "I love you."

Brenner moved closer to her almost naked body. "I love you too."

Abby settled into bed with Brenner by her side and together they let the hours slip into morning. By daybreak, Abby had decided to talk with the members of the covenant and beg them to make him whole again.

This time, forever.

CHAPTER NINETEEN

The day after the big event, the covenant gathered together at the airport before boarding their planes for their home destinations.

Destiny hugged each person good-bye and announced loudly, "Thanks everyone, for coming!"

They all agreed that it was a blast and that they should get together again soon.

"Next time, let's not make it only for two hours", someone laughed at their own joke.

Her own laughter jogged her memory and then it didn't seem as funny anymore. Destiny suddenly remembered how Brenner died and why. She had a thought and hushed everyone to listen, then gathered them around her. She quickly explained her idea to the members of the covenant. "So, what do you all think? Should we?"

They talked about it as a group and then decided that perhaps they should convene once more. They quickly agreed.

At the impromptu meeting an hour later, everyone decided that two hours was not enough time for the lovers to be together. Brenner in this life was the way that it should be. They all concurred that he was to spend eternity in the arms of the one he loves – Abby.

The covenant talked some more and came up with a plan. They decided that because Brenner killed himself from grief, he left this Earth long before his proper time.

Because of the proven strong love between Abby and Brenner, the covenant of powerful witches and soothsayers had to decide if they should keep him on Earth to live out his final days.

"If yes, a new spell needed to be worked out and plans had to be made", Destiny declared. "Perhaps we should convene once more in a proper, more formal meeting?"

They all looked at each other and knew that Destiny was right. Two hours was not enough when the love was this real.

Flights were cancelled and the next meeting was scheduled for the following afternoon. Everyone dispersed and was asked to bring back a spell, and other suggestions, that could work to bring him to life.

When the meeting was over, Destiny called Melissa's cell phone and told her what had transpired at the airport.

"Are you kidding?" Melissa was deliriously happy. She couldn't believe the strange turn of events that had taken place. She wished that she could have been there to witness it.

Destiny asked Melissa for her attendance and told her the time that they would all be meeting the next day.

"You bet I'll be there!"

Melissa, out doing a little last-minute shopping, exploded with happiness and couldn't wait to tell Abby. She called her sister right away.

"Really?" Abby was almost speechless. She turned to Brenner and let him know the news. She watched as he smiled. She then turned her attention back to Melissa. "Do you want us to come too?"

"I'm not sure. Can you watch Echo for me tomorrow? If we need you to come, you can always bring her along."

"Absolutely!" Abby turned to Brenner who she knew would be thrilled to keep Echo's company.

"Fabulous!"

The next day, the same 6 women and 2 men were called upon to sit at the large, oval table.

Sylveeno was grateful to spend another day or two with Melissa. He found her intriguing, delightful, and full of spirit. They would talk again after the meeting; he would make sure of it.

He could see that things were about to start, so Sylveeno pushed his thoughts to the back of his mind until the meeting was done and over with.

Destiny clapped her hands together and shouted for their attention. "This meeting will now come to order." She watched as everyone quieted down and turned towards her.

The whole meeting focused on the new spell. They talked about what each of them had learned from other spells of this magnitude, and what they needed to make this new spell happen. The more they talked, the more they realized how much power this will use. After a while, they knew that they required more help than what was gathered in this room.

Because a spell like this takes a lot of power, thought, and energy, they all agreed that a much higher person had to be present for this next incantation to be performed. A spell of this degree does not get performed often, for a number of reasons.

The covenant also needed permission to perform this spell of which they were struggling with. It must be for a distinctive purpose, and it must be because of an extraordinary circumstance.

They talked for hours and then all came to the same conclusion. It was decided that the covenant will call upon Hilary Tussaud.

Hilary was the highest and most powerful person that they could all think of. She was a true witch, becoming one after she was banned from six different countries for trying to kill her husband.

Hilary was married off to an unknown man who came to her home one night and who was then terribly brutal to her during the two years of their marriage. She hated him so much that she learned to do magic from an old lady in the woods. She had little money so the old woman asked for what she could afford to pay, plus a year of her life. The young woman agreed in an instant.

Hilary learned a spell to slowly poison her husband day-by-day, but he found out a week later. He made Hilary tell him how she made him sick and who had helped her. Then he beat her until she couldn't walk.

The old woman had a sixth sense and felt terrible. She knew it had something to do with her young friend, Hilary, and she wanted to help. She took out her Tarot cards and laid them down one at-a-time. The cards explained what had happened and why. After some careful thought, the frail old female knew what had to be done.

The old woman waited until the husband was out at work and then rescued her friend from her terrible life. The husband came home and was surprised to find that his wife was not there. He knew immediately where she might have gone.

Mr. Rafferty showed up at the old dame's home and demanded to have his wife back. The old woman laughed in his face and then lay such a horrible, painful spell on him, that he happily took his own life a few days later.

Hilary recovered quickly, thanks to the frail woman and her home remedies. Hilary sold her modest abode that she once shared with her husband, and came to live with the old woman in her shack of a house.

For years they stood side-by-side in the small kitchen as Hilary learned powerful magic and did small and large spells. She even tried her hand at growing the ingredients that were needed to perform them. Pretty soon, all the people who came asking for favors and spells of the old woman, asked for Hilary instead.

Hilary was given a small amount of money, plus one year of life for each spell that she performed. As the years went by, Hilary became stronger and more powerful.

The elderly wench hadn't been given more years to her life in a long while, so she slowly became frail and weak. As with everything, time runs out. The old woman eventually died leaving all of her powers and belongings to Hilary.

Hilary stayed in the rickety home, and from the old lady's books and notes, she learned more and more about witchcraft and magic. She kept performing spells and granting wishes and has lived a wonderful and fulfilled life from then until now.

Hilary got called, and after hearing the story, accepted the invitation. She arrived the next day.

All the members of the covenant rose to their feet when

Hilary entered the room. The group smiled and watched as she sat down at the head of the table.

Each person present, held the utmost respect for the highest person of power in the room. Each one at the table has asked at least one question of Hilary in the past, and each one had been bestowed an answer or a gift.

Hilary got introduced to everyone around the table and remembered these people from before. What was asked from most of them was more power and knowledge. The having to give something in return, was extra years onto Hilary's lifespan.

Hilary recalled all of these people who had come from around the world, asking for help in their relationships, health, wealth, and work life. She granted each and every request, asking only a year of their life in exchange to give them a better one.

Hilary sat in the seat of honor while everyone else took a seat around the table and waited for the meeting to convene. This time it was Hilary who did the clapping. "This meeting will now come to order."

Destiny and Sylveeno did most of the talking for the future spell. Rosalyn and Ariel told Hilary the details about the last spell and the situation of the two people. Dominic thanked Hilary for her attendance and then provided everyone with his idea for a new spell. Melissa sat and watched.

Hilary asked a few questions while she heard the plight of the two young lovers in question: how he died, how they met, and how they want to spend their lives together.

Satisfied with what she had heard so far, Hilary nodded

in agreement at the request of the two of them living together in this century. "I strongly believe that we can do this, IF the love is as strong as you state it is."

Hilary turned to Destiny and asked for the couple to join the meeting.

Destiny nodded in Melissa's direction and then watched as she quietly left the room. Once she was out in the hall, Melissa pulled out her cell phone and invited Abby to the meeting.

"They want to give Brenner permanent life!" she exclaimed as quietly as she could.

Abby was dumbstruck. She couldn't believe it. This was her wish, what she wanted more than anything. "Okay, what do you want me to do?"

"They want you at the meeting. Can you come?"

Abby turned around and listened for the direction of the laughter which was coming from Echo. "I have to bring your daughter with me."

Melissa lowered her eyes. She was not sure how that would go over, but Abby needed to be here so she conceded. "You have to bring her. We have no other choice."

Abby thought about her mom, but then realized there was no time. "We'll be right there."

Destiny poked her head out to see how it was going. She watched as Melissa nodded that Abby was on her way. "Remind her of the agreement of giving up one year of her life."

Abby heard the statement through the phone and replied

happily. "If you could make this happen," she exclaimed, "You could have anything you want from me."

"That's what we want to hear. See you soon." Melissa was beside herself with excitement; to be with these powerful people, to be part of such a huge spell, and to do something as great as this for her baby sister.

The two women went back inside to the meeting which was still in progress. The group was talking about a spell that they thought would work.

As Melissa sat down, she could feel someone watching her closer than she would have liked. She scanned the room but no-one's eyes were upon her. How odd, she remarked to herself.

Sylveeno felt such a need to speak with Melissa, but kept his thoughts and feelings to himself for another little while.

Hilary applauded Dominic's spell, which would bring life to a former human being. She stood up and used the white board to show the facts behind it.

"First we need to gather rain water from the storm during the next full moon", she began. "Any rain water, from any storm, just will not work. Keep the water fresh in the fridge until the day of the spell. The spell must then be performed on the 2nd day of the following full moon."

Roxanne's hand went up immediately and everyone could see that she was quite excited. Hilary pointed in her direction as Dominic checked the schedule of the moon.

"I'm sorry to interrupt you, Miss Hilary, but I have enough rain water in my possession to perform this spell tomorrow, if you'd like." Roxanne listened to the gasps and small chatter in the room and watched as everyone became very animated.

Hilary was overwhelmed. Then she remembered that rain water from a full moon gives the hair strength and shine. The rain water from a full moon also adds 'glue' to many spells, so it was no wonder that at least one person in the room had a small amount with them.

"Very good!" she shouted. Using her fingers, she listed off a few more things that were needed.

Dominic tried to get Hilary's attention while she was in mid-sentence. He watched as she slowly turned to look in his direction and nodded for him to go ahead. "The next full moon is in three days", he stated.

Hilary was not thrilled to be interrupted, but now felt proud of the very efficient people in the room.

"Wonderful!" she shouted. She went back to her blackboard, rushing now as her time was more limited than she had previously thought. She bullet-formed a list of things that she needed to have, or have done, in order to do this spell.

"We need a photo or hand-drawing of the two people in question. We need to find a spot outside where we can all sit in a circle. We need to find large, bright flowers to place in the four corners to represent the north, east, west, and south quadrants." She paused and turned from the wall to sit down.

"Once we have our items", she continued. "We need to place the bowl of rain water and a candle, in the middle of our circle so we are all facing it. We shall light the candle and allow it to burn until the water extinguishes it. While it is burning, we have a chant we must say."

Hilary grabbed her briefcase and leafed through it, trying to find the sheet that she needed. "Got it!" she proclaimed after struggling for a few seconds.

As Hilary was handing out the paper that held the words to the chant, she continued speaking. "We could also put a stick of incense behind each person in the circle to aid the helpers of our intention."

Helpers are entities who have passed on but are willing to guide others in the quest for spells or life.

The room was semi-quiet as everyone was sitting at the large oval table reading the words on the papers that were handed out.

The knock on the door startled everyone, but announced the arrival of Abby and Brenner. Destiny stood up to let them in.

CHAPTER TWENTY

Chapter Twenty

Hilary's heart started pounding wildly when she spotted a vague image of Brenner enter the room. Her eyes were wide with bewilderment and confusion. She was told what the meeting was about, but was not given any names.

Letting out a silent gasp, she placed her hands flat on the table and moved her body forward, bracing herself to stand-up.

Brenner came in behind Abby. They were asked to be seated in a certain spot at the oval table. As Brenner's eyes scanned the room, he came across Hilary and he locked eyes with her.

Hilary quickly removed her hands and sat back in her chair. She couldn't think. Brenner was still as handsome as he was the last time she had set eyes on him. Would he remember her, she wondered.

Hilary unlocked eyes with him and immediately lowered her gaze so he wouldn't recognize her.

Brenner watched the woman who lowered her head towards the table. He felt an immediate familiarity with her but couldn't place why. Sylveeno started speaking so Brenner moved his focus in that direction and tried to pay attention.

Hilary hadn't thought about him in decades. One minute she was having a wonderful time with this very handsome man, and the next night she was married off to a stranger.

Hilary had often wondered why Brenner's mother brought Mr. Rafferty to marry her. She also wondered why Brenner had not stopped it from happening.

A lady-like knock came hard upon the front door late one night. Hilary was ordered by her father to open it. There she found Brenner's parents and a man whom she had never met.

"Good evening, Miss Hilary", Lilliana said as she gracefully extended her left hand in a sweeping motion to bring the strange man to her attention. "You know my husband, and this is Mr. Rafferty."

Hilary paused and made a slight courtesy. Them calling at such a late hour did not seem regular, but she politely invited them inside her home. As she moved aside to allow them entrance, her father called from behind her.

"What is it?" he inquired from the other room. "Who could be calling at this hour?" He stepped into the parlor and found three people waiting for his attention.

"Good evening, dear sir", said Lilliana as she brought her hand to meet his. "You remember my husband, and this is our friend, Mr. Rafferty." She turned and waited for them all to shake hands. "Would it be proper for us to have a few moments of your time, kind sir?"

Hilary's father looked at his daughter, hoping that she would know what this was about. When it was apparent that she did not, he asked them to follow him into the sitting room, a few feet from where they stood.

After everyone was seated, Lilliana asked if they could be alone. When it was acknowledged that Hilary's father did not understand that she meant for them to meet without his daughter, Lilliana spoke up. "Hilary, dear", she ordered passively. "Would you mind getting us some tea?"

Hilary looked towards her father and he towards her. He

was very confused, but gave his permission for her to get the tea.

"Right away, father." She curtsied as she spoke.

Hilary dashed out of the room but stopped after the first wall. She wanted to be sure that she was close enough to hear every word that was about to be spoken.

When they were alone, Lilliana verbalized her intentions in no uncertain terms. "Dear sir", she declared towards Hilary's father. "My friend needs a wife and we all thought immediately of your lovely daughter."

Hilary's father, knowing that she was fond of Brenner, started fussing with his hands in his laps. "But I thought she was spoken for", he commented with a bit of concern. He couldn't help but wonder if Brenner's parents knew that the two youngsters were seeing each other.

Lilliana knew this would take work, but she was prepared. "Dear sir", she began as she turned towards the stranger in the room.

"Our friend here has money in his pocket to make this quite profitable for you, should you accept. He has seen your daughter buying one of my wares, and fell in love with her immediately. He asked me for her name and I gave it. He then asked to meet you."

Hilary's hands raced to her mouth. She wanted to scream but knew she shouldn't. She needed to hear what her father's response would be so she crept a bit closer to the door frame and listened while holding her breath.

Being terribly low on money, Hilary's father moved the ends of his mustache with the forefinger on his left hand. He stood up and slowly paced the floor with his other hand across his lower back. He muddled the proposition for a few minutes and thought about the age of his daughter. Then he thought about what the money would mean to his land and future.

Lilliana grabbed her husband's hand and wished for her plan to work. She squeezed his fingers tightly together and prayed like she'd never prayed before. She watched as the pacing man stopped and stood in front of the stranger in the room.

Charles tapped his free hand over his wife's shaking one, to reassure her that everything would be okay.

Hilary's father stood directly in front of Mr. Rafferty and extended his right hand. "Congratulations, son."

Mr. Rafferty stood up and placed his free hand on his father-in-law's shoulder. They laughed a hearty, deep laugh while the parents of Brenner stood up and joined in the fun. Mr. Rafferty removed a white envelope from the inside of his jacket and handed it to Hilary's father.

The envelope was very thick and father guessed there could be a thousand dollars held within its confines. This made him very pleased. The deal was now complete.

Lilliana was beside herself with happiness. Mr. Rafferty, after seeing the daughter again, was thrilled. Hilary wanted to faint, cry, and scream. She had no intention of marrying anyone but Brenner.

"Hilary!"

Hilary pulled herself together when she heard her father's strong voice calling for her presence. She came dashing into the room holding both sides of her long dress. "Yes, father", she said politely, dreading what he was about to convey. She knew that he was going to announce her wedding to the stranger but she wanted to have more time. Her mind started swimming with reasons why she could not get married.

Father walked over to his new son-in-law and put his arms around his shoulders. "Hilary!" he called for her to come to his other side. "Come and meet your husband."

Hilary choked and her feet didn't want to move, but she managed to saunter over to the happy groom-to-be. All her reasons for not getting married swam away, never to return.

With her father on one side and her groom on the other, this couldn't have been a more awkward moment for Hilary. Her thoughts were on Brenner and them running away together somewhere far away, where no-one could ever find them.

Lilliana was beside herself and couldn't wait for the next bit of news. She hushed everyone to silence for her next announcement. "Since my husband is a preacher, we can have the wedding right away." She clapped her hands as she spoke, hoping to move things along more rapidly.

Mr. Rafferty grabbed both sides of his lapel and puffed out his chest. "Yes", he agreed. "The quicker the better as I have business in town the day after tomorrow. My wife can come with me and we can start our new life right away."

Mr. Rafferty turned towards Hilary's father and waited for his opinion.

Father was terribly surprised that the wedding would be so quick. He certainly hadn't prepared for this. He turned and looked into Hilary's terrified face. He then knew that if she had a few days to think about it, she would never do it.

Hilary's father patted the thick envelope in his front pocket and recognized what he had to do.

He turned to his only daughter, and with tears hidden behind his eyes, he grabbed both of her shoulders and spoke. "Hilary", he began as his heart broke. "He seems like a good man. He will make you a good husband. You will never have to live poor again."

Hilary broke free from her father's clutches and ran across the room. "But father", she pleaded. "I am not in love with him." She turned towards her father with great speed. "How can I marry a man that I am not in love with?"

Mr. Rafferty spoke up and walked towards his bride-to-be. "You will learn to love me in time, my dear", he stated as if he had authority on the subject. "You will have all the money you wish, a home, servants, and land. You will want for nothing, but a child." He turned and chuckled in the direction of the men in the room. He then looked back into Hilary's face. "In time, I shall give you that as well." He raised his index finger in her direction and shook it while laughing. "Now, no more fussing. Let us marry and be off."

Hilary hated him from that moment on. She turned towards Lilliana and hoped that she would understand, her being a woman and all. Hilary had no idea that this whole thing was Lilliana's way of freeing Brenner from a penniless woman such as herself.

Hilary and her father may not have a lot of money, but they were good folk; decent and hard working. She knew in her heart that she would have made Brenner a good wife, but now she'll never get the chance to prove it.

Lilliana's spirit was floating high above the clouds with happiness. Once she was free of Hilary, her son would have his pick of all the girls in the land. She knew that her son would not be happy at first when he learns about Hilary getting married and running off, but time heals all and he would soon get over it. Of that, she was certain.

Hilary was more than devastated but not sure what to do next. With everyone on Mr. Rafferty's side, she lowered her head and gave in. While everyone around her cheered her decision, she felt empty and cold.

The ceremony took place immediately and the wine, which Lilliana brought with her, was poured. Hilary's glass, which was to be sipped, was guzzled as quickly as possible. She then turned and ran to her room. Lilliana followed.

Brenner's mother helped Hilary pack while explaining that this was the better choice for her. Mr. Rafferty would be able to provide for her like no other man could.

Hilary turned and looked straight into Lilliana's face. "I love your son", she said with tears streaming down her cheeks. "I love him and he loves me back. We could make a fine life together."

Not one to be defeated, Lilliana burst into Hilary's face. "He does not love you, Hilary", she shot with anger. "He cannot and will not be yours. You have a fine man as your husband. Go with him and be happy."

Hilary's heart broke even more. She turned away and shed more tears at the words that Lilliana spat out. How could he not love me, she debated to herself. We spend everyday together laughing and talking about our future.

Lilliana finished the packing and escorted Hilary out to say good-bye to her father, and to thank the minister for the lovely service.

As the front door opened and the newly married couple were about to leave, Hilary turned and looked once more into Lilliana's face to be sure that what they had spoken about was true. When Hilary saw nothing in the older woman's eyes but contempt, she sadly went with her husband to his very stately carriage.

Lilliana and Charles said their good-byes to the two men and bid Hilary good luck on her new marriage. They entered their carriage and made a quick exit towards home.

After Hilary was seated, she looked towards her childhood home as her father stood on their small, wooden porch, and waved his hand in their direction, biding them good-bye and good luck. Although she obeyed him, even when her heart was not in it, she hated her father for letting this happen tonight. He needed the money and Hilary knew that, but it was a poor excuse for marrying off your only child.

As the horses started their march towards town, Hilary watched as her father collapsed onto the ground by the front door. She screamed and wanted to get out of the moving carriage to help him, but her husband stopped her. He rushed the horses faster and soon they were out of sight.

The sad man cried as he held his old weathered face in his hands. He prayed that his daughter would be okay and that one day she would forgive him. As he remembered her sad face during the ceremony, Hilary's father wondered if he had done the right thing.

That was the last time Hilary saw her father. He died two days later.

CHAPTER TWENTY-ONE

Hilary raised her eyes to see her beloved Brenner again. She had never been sure if what had happened was what Brenner wanted, or someone else.

Over the years, she tried to find him once she was free of her husband, but she didn't know where he was. After a few years of searching, she stopped but her heart never let go. Now he was here and she didn't know what to do.

The reason Hilary could not find Brenner was because he had died: He was no longer on this Earth as a human being. Hilary used powerful spells and magic to bring a living soul to her side, not a ghost or other entity. Had she known the truth, things might have been different.

All these feelings were consuming Hilary and she couldn't think straight. Would she truly give Brenner life so he could be with another woman, she wondered. Am I that strong?

Abby was amazed at everything that was being said and done for her benefit. All of these people were in this very room to help her and Brenner be together forever. She was beside herself with happiness.

Abby's eyes scanned the room and quietly blessed each and every soul for coming here. She spotted a woman whose head was bent down and facing the table rather than looking up and at the head master who was speaking. She wondered why this was, but ignored the woman when she heard her own name being said.

Destiny was more than privileged to be part of this group. She had a lot to offer and was the person who originally started this whole ball rolling. Of course she would be present during this once-in-a-lifetime moment. She was officially invited by Hilary to attend and participate, and was honored and delighted at the invitation.

All of a sudden Brenner's mind popped. He moved quickly and looked over at Hilary's face and suddenly remembered how he knew her.

Hilary could feel the hairs on the back of her neck and arms stand straight up and she knew that Brenner was staring at her. She looked up and caught his icy glance. She knew from his expression that he had now remembered who she was.

Brenner didn't know what to do. Do I speak, he wondered. Can it really be her, he doubted.

Brenner locked eyes with Hilary and tried to get her to speak with him from within. "Do I know you?" he asked through mental telepathy.

Hilary was overjoyed that he remembered her. "Yes", she answered while nodding her head ever so slightly. Her eyes glistened as they started to water. She tried to hold back the tears so no-one else in the room knew what was happening.

"We go back a long way", she said as she smiled and thanked the stars that he was in the same room as her.

Brenner couldn't believe his eyes. His first love from so long ago was really here with him. "So, how is this possible?"

Hilary, still being able to hear his words in her mind, answered by closing her eyes and sending him the entire three years of her life, from the moment his mother entered her father's home, to the day that the old woman passed away.

When Hilary opened her eyes again, she saw that Brenner had shed a few tears of his own. She felt his heart had slowed down and he was now in despair for her. She watched as he took a step backwards and closed his own eyes. "I'm so sorry for you. I didn't know. I'm sending you a hug."

Hilary suddenly felt a huge warmness gather tight around her body. She felt enveloped and calm, and more emotion than she had ever experienced in her life. This feeling seemed to fill her entire being, inside and out. It left her feeling dizzy and very loved.

Brenner spoke to Hilary again using mental telepathy. "I am the way I am now because I was so distraught that you had married another, that I took my own life. I learned what my mother had done and was angry at her for interfering. I had hoped that she would feel the same pain from me dying, as she gave to my heart when I heard that you had wed."

Brenner went on and poured out his love for Hilary and pleaded his apology for killing himself. He wanted her to know that he would have loved her forever, had he had the chance. "What I did, was done out of a moment's anger", he continued. "Had I to do it over again, I would seek you out, Hilary, and ask you to run away with me."

Hilary opened her eyes and thanked him. "We were both so young."

Brenner agreed.

Hilary was so moved and wanted to cry. She wanted to rush over and embrace him, but in that moment was not the time. She now knew that he had nothing to do with her marriage to Mr. Rafferty. It changed her prospective on the world, and her feelings towards people in general.

Hilary turned her attention to the rest of the group and cleared her throat as she was about to speak. She had decided that no matter what the rest of the covenant was going to do, she was going to give life to Brenner to make up for him losing his. She felt a bit guilty for him ending his life for her. Now she will give him a gift to say thank you for the same reason.

As she moved to look into Abby's face, Hilary's mind was already percolating. She was going to use the most powerful spell that she had in her possession to bring Brenner back to life. She looked around the table and knew that with the people contained within this room, she could make this work.

Hilary was about to speak but her body froze when she heard her mother's voice in her head saying, "And a small child shall lead them."

Hilary could feel a lump forming in her throat when the words were spoken somewhere in the back of her mind. She felt a chill run up her back and an incredible warmness swished all around her. She could smell her mother's hair and the feel of her hands against her cheek, and she wanted so much to call out her name.

Hilary's mother had passed away when she was very young but she remembered so many things about the loving woman – how tall she was, how caring, and how very attentive she was to her only daughter. Throughout the years, Hilary's mother did not 'speak' to her often, but when she did, Hilary listened.

The voice today was so strong and very clear in Hilary's mind.

It was as if her mother was standing beside her, guiding her, helping her to fulfill this one last immeasurable spell.

Hilary closed her eyes and brought both her hands up to her chest. She crossed her arms as she thanked her mother and blessed her spirit for being in the room. "Thanks, mom."

Hilary felt quiet inside now. She suddenly felt totally at peace. She opened her eyes and wanted to continue with her task at hand.

This next spell would take up a lot of her energy and she wondered if it might be her last one.

Hilary knew that her days were dwindling and it made her sad. She hadn't done any real spells or magic in a long time so it made this event more exciting and even more challenging.

Hilary had not sustained herself the way she should have and this particular spell will take a lot of power from her body.

If and when she died, everything would go with her. Hilary knew that if her powers and knowledge were to carry on, there must be someone out there who could take over, but she hadn't met the person yet.

Echo Prudence Hudson burst into the room where the covenant was being held and stood beside her mother, begging for her attention.

Sylveeno watched as the mother and daughter interacted. He now wondered about the child's father.

Hilary's thoughts disappeared as she quickly turned to look in Melissa's direction, as did the entire congregation.

Melissa hushed Echo to silence and hugged her close

to her body hoping that nobody was distracted by the interruption.

Hilary looked first at Melissa and then into Echo's young face. She was terribly surprised to find that herself and the young child seemed to have a strong connection, even from across the room.

Echo felt something strange, an oddness close by, and then turned her head to find it. Her inner radar pointed her across the room as her eyes stared in Hilary's direction.

Echo was not surprised when she saw that the woman was also looking at her. Echo was not sure why this woman attracted so much power, but she couldn't seem to break away.

The room and all the people in it, the noise, the chatter, and the ambience, all seemed to disappear when the connection was made. When their eyes locked, their power was the strongest.

Hilary could feel the pull, the magic that poured from the tiny body. She took one look at the beautiful, blonde-haired child and knew instantly that she was the next one to take over her powers.

Hilary wasn't sure how she got here or who she belonged to, but that didn't seem to matter in this instant. She needed to test her ability to be sure. Hilary bid the child to come over using nothing but her mind.

Echo, who was still watching Hilary, heard the plea in her mind and without blinking, walked over to Hilary's chair. She greeted her as if they had known each other all their lives. They embraced and the affiliation and power was felt by everyone in the room.

While the alliance was not yet broken, the room became alive with talking and noises. Everyone wanted to know what was going on between the head witch and the small child. All eyes and attention were now focused around Hilary's chair.

Melissa was very pleased and proud because she had always sensed that her daughter had a gift. She couldn't be happier that she was right and that the highest person in power on the planet, could also feel it.

Echo sensed that there was something different about Hilary, even before she was told. Not having ever met Hilary before, Echo went over to her left side and sat down on the chair. Their eyes were still locked and their minds were still connected.

Abby was wondering if Echo was a distraction and should be called away from Hilary. Inwardly, she was afraid of what was happening and if it would have something to do with the next spell.

After a few seconds of personal assessing, Hilary could feel that this little girl was indeed the one. She reached out and stroked her soft hair, then looked over at Melissa. "You are her mother?"

"Yes, Madam Hilary." Melissa stood up and smiled proudly.

"And where is the father?"

Melissa became embarrassed and didn't want to answer. She didn't want the world to know that her daughter had come from a short-lived affair.

Echo spoke up in her mother's place. "I don't have one, Madam Hilary."

Melissa secretly blessed her child for coming to her rescue. She never felt it was a tragedy not to have a man in their lives, for Echo didn't want for anything. Melissa was a great provider and loved her daughter more than she loved her own life.

Sylveeno smiled with this new lot of information.

"We shall speak later." Hilary turned her attention back to the child sitting next to her.

Echo turned away for a very brief moment and looked for Brenner. She found him standing behind Abby's chair. Upon seeing his handsome face, she smiled and said HI to him via mental telepathy.

Brenner always knew that there was something special about the little girl. He smiled back and said HI to his young friend, using nothing but his mind.

Echo turned her attention towards Hilary again.

Hilary saw the interaction between Brenner and Echo and now knew for sure that the little girl had extraordinary powers. She was more than pleased to have Echo take over for her.

Hilary decided that she needed a few minutes and adjourned the meeting.

After everyone got up, Melissa was taken aside and Hilary explained her plan to give Echo all that she had to offer. Echo could continue her normal, everyday routine, but must come to Hilary's home on the week-ends so that she could learn everything there was to know.

Melissa was very proud and agreed without hesitation. She looked to Echo who also loved the idea. They talked for a few more minutes and then decided to reconvene the meeting, keeping Echo and Melissa on either side of Hilary.

Hilary clapped her hands as she spoke. "Let us continue."

A large paper was sprawled out on the conference table and everyone looked to check out the next full moon, the longitude and latitude of the area they had chosen to chant the spell, and the position of the planets and stars.

Hilary was very pleased to inform her members that, "According to our calculations, we can proceed in three days as stated by Dominic, but our last meeting will be held in two." She smiled as everyone clapped and cheered in great delight.

They discussed a few more details and an hour later, the meeting was adjourned and everyone went their own way.

Because the site of the next spell must be performed in Canmore, a small leap from Banff, the group decided to rent rooms in the large hotel in the middle of town. Melissa and Abby decided not to stay in the hotel, but instead rented a small cabin very close to where the others were staying.

Echo slept in the big bedroom after she made Brenner promise to sleep there too. Melissa and Abby slept on the couches in the living room and ended up talking for most of the night.

First thing the next morning, Hilary went to the nearby river and walked beside it. Eventually, she took out a small, brown, leather satchel. She dipped her fingers in and took out a handful of fresh tobacco which she then sprinkled sparsely into the rapidly flowing water. She did this in a circular motion while saying thank you to the Gods above for blessing the union of Brenner and Abby.

Hilary did this three more times and then placed the satchel on the ground beside her left foot. She raised her hands - palms up, and her face - eyes closed, to the morning sun and prayed silently. She let the light warm her face and body, energizing her spirit and giving her the inner strength that she will need for this next and last spell.

A half hour passed and Hilary was then done with her preparations. She said thank you out loud as she blew a kiss to the water, the air, and the earth. She then looked to the sky and blew a kiss from her open hand to the heavens above. She felt that everything was now perfect, and she could leave the area.

She went back to her hotel room and spent the rest of the day chanting and praying, hoping that all will work out as planned.

The next morning, Hilary left her hotel room and prepared herself for a full, all-over body massage, then a steam bath. This not only cleansed her physically, but spiritually as well. In the late afternoon, she got ready to meet with Melissa and Echo in the downstairs restaurant.

Melissa arrived with Echo and both were quite excited to have the visit with Hilary. They talked about Echo's powers – when they began and how strong they were now. Melissa was also questioned about her own powers – what she had learned since she was a teen and why.

Hilary was fascinated by both the mother and the daughter, and by the end of their visit, she truly believed in their powers. Hilary was now more convinced than ever that Echo will be the one to take over her reign when she was gone.

Once their lunch was over, Hilary gave them both a ritual blessing and bid them good-bye.

On day three, as Hilary arrived in the Bellamy Room on the main floor of the hotel, she took a head count and saw that almost everyone had arrived. She clapped her hands together to get their attention and then gathered everyone around her. The covenant waited until Hilary was seated before they took their own seat.

Everyone wondered why Echo was not only in the room, but sitting on Hilary's left side again.

"As you can see", Hilary began with her arms out and open wide. "The little one has now joined our group. After a lot of careful study, I believe that she has the power to take over all of my spells and power once I'm gone. I believe with all my soul that Echo will eventually be even stronger than I."

The room went quiet and everyone looked at Echo. They all watched as she beamed first at her mother, and then in Hilary's direction.

Melissa was very proud and smiled as only a mother could in this type of situation.

Questions were allowed and asked right away. Answers were given by both Melissa and Hilary. Once everyone was satisfied with what they were told, the meeting went in another direction…. the spell.

Hilary announced that the spell will be performed the next day and what it entailed. "This time, Echo gets to stay." Hilary placed a loving hand over Echo's small one.

The little girl proudly sat between Melissa and Hilary, now holding each of their hands.

The entire covenant knew enough not to question the unknowns of whys or hows. Each person in the group congratulated the young child in all her future endeavors. They wished her well and bestowed upon her much love.

Echo's face blossomed with a huge smile. "Thank you for your kind thoughts."

Echo turned to her mother and Hilary, then to Abby and Brenner. She felt very excited for this is what she had always dreamed of – having more power and one day performing her own spells for people.

After an hour of discussing and planning the next day's events, Hilary ended the day's meeting. Everyone was very excited and couldn't wait to be part of the magnificent event.

CHAPTER TWENTY-TWO

At precisely 10am, the members of the covenant came one-by-one into the area chosen to perform the spell. When the last person arrived, the meeting began.

Brenner stayed in the cabin. He did his own wishing and praying that this powerful spell would work. He closed his eyes at the scheduled time and thought about all the things that he could do, if only he was alive.

Abby was placed in the middle of the group, standing still and looking up. She was dressed in a long-flowing, purple outfit, flowers in her hair, and a smile upon her face. She was told to keep her arms out, palms up, her heart full of love, and her mind open. She was not to chant with the rest of the group, but merely listen and pray with all her might that the spell works.

With Echo in attendance, the group was now complete; standing, and ready to perform the greatest spell of the century.

"Really believe in what you are saying!" Hilary shouted with a burst of energy. She wanted this to work for Brenner. She wanted to give her all for this one last spell.

As the covenant closed their eyes and chanted the words to the spell, the slow swirling air around them became thicker. The energy changed and a kind of whirlwind started in a small corner of the circle surrounding them.

Sacred water here it be
To draw him very near
As endless rivers rush to sea
Make his path ever clear

Everyone was focused on why they are doing the spell. The more power they felt, the better they were encouraged that it would work.

"Louder!" Hilary yelled. "Really dig into your soul as you shout!"

> **True love once here he'll find**
> **His journey now has an end**
> **And in his heart and soul and mind**
> **He'll know their lives should blend**

The chanting now continued on a louder level. The power increased and everyone felt it. This was stronger than anything anyone in the circle had ever done before. Everyone could feel the drain and strain on their bodies and souls, but they knew enough to continue.

> **By the time the flame is out**
> **The spell will have been set**
> **And there could never be a doubt**
> **That our wishes won't be met**

Another moment later, the spell had been cast and everyone leaned forward from exhaustion. They grabbed their chests and knees, or fell to the ground for support. They agreed that this has certainly been the best spell any of them had ever done in their lives.

During the last ten minutes or so, Brenner felt the many changes that were happening to his body. This time it was more powerful and more pronounced than before. He felt different, like he could run forever and never have to stop. He felt inspired and totally consumed with love. He could feel his heart beating and this scared him, for he didn't want it to break again.

When the strange sensations in the room went away, and the ground below his feet stopped grumbling, Brenner stood up and made fists with his hands. He was whole again, but this time he knew it would be forever. He couldn't wait to show Abby.

Drained and exhausted, the covenant headed back to the board room. When they arrived, Abby looked into each and every face of the dear people that had helped her. She watched as some struggled with the small task of walking or sitting down. She shed tears of joy that these people did this for her.

Abby tried to grab all of their attention by saying a huge thank you to the group. "Thanks everyone for today!" Even if they could not hear or comprehend what she was saying, she said it again. "Thank You!"

Brenner had arrived and came inside the building. He now had to find his sweetheart. When he heard Abby's voice, he followed the trail.

As the members of the covenant tried to lift their heads with acknowledgement of Abby's words, they noticed something remarkable coming through the semi-open door. Everyone was astounded and turned to look.

Brenner, as clear as can be, could now be seen and heard by everyone attending. He smiled with delight as his eyes scanned the room looking for Abby.

Abby felt an odd sensation, which went up her back and

made her grin from ear-to-ear. She turned towards the door and saw Brenner in full form. Her face beamed as she realized the spell had worked. She ran in his direction and stood face-to-face with him as the room full of people laughed with excitement.

With both her hands embracing and caressing his face, she cried happy tears. "Are you really alive?" she asked.

"I've never been more alive", he whispered sensuously within an inch of Abby's face.

Abby jumped up and into his arms and they kissed like two teenagers in love as the group clapped and cheered them on.

The feeling of being human again was overwhelming and too real to believe. Brenner's mind was overloading with the realization that he could now hug and kiss Abby whenever he wanted. He loved that others could now see him and they all liked what they saw.

Brenner grabbed Abby tighter and didn't want to let go.

As they embraced, Brenner looked over Abby's shoulder and directly into Hilary's face. He saw her watery eyes and knew that she was sad, but happy at the same time. He shed a tear for her and then thanked Hilary for the greatest gift one could ever have.

Using only his mind he said, "I will love you forever, Hilary."

Hilary smiled, shed another tear, and then nodded with acknowledgement in his direction. If she couldn't have him, then he should at least be happy with the one he loved now.

"I will always love you too."

THE REST OF THEIR LIVES

Having Brenner alive in this day and age, brought a newness to Abby that she never thought possible. Not only was she happier than she'd ever dreamed of, but every single thing that they did together, was a first.

Abby saw the world through Brenner's eyes and loved it. Cars, malls, buildings, the lights, the people, the hustle and bustle, music, TV and radio. Things that she used to take for granted, now made her happy to experience.

Brenner loved this gift of a new life in this century, and was pleased to be able to enjoy it for many years to come.

Abby and Brenner stayed living in the old farmhouse, only he moved his things downstairs and now slept in the master bedroom with Abby, who was only to happy to share.

Their first night together as man and wife was truly magical. They made love for the second time, and this time they created a baby.

Nine months later, they had a child – a girl who they named, Cherity Annabelle Jaxon. They were thrilled as they both got to watch her grow up and get married.

Abby and Brenner consulted Destiny on the eve of every Halloween. She gave them hope and advice for the following 12 months. They listened and followed her words of wisdom and were able to have a long and very happy life together.

Hilary also stayed a big fixture in the Jaxon's lives. She not only became a Godmother to their only child, but she became best friends with Brenner's wife, Abby.

Hilary was very moved that she was able to grant Brenner

the gift of life, a once-in-a-lifetime spell, but it took a lot out of her. Sadly, Hilary only lived for another 14 years.

Echo lived with Hilary on as many week-ends as was possible while growing up. She learned quickly and eventually took over all of Hilary's powers and clients. As she approached her twentieth birthday, she became the most powerful magical person on earth.

Sylveeno finally asked Melissa out for coffee on the day when Brenner became human again. She said yes and they dated for one year before getting married and starting a family. Echo now has two younger brothers who, happily, have no powers at all.

Brenner lived another 46 years and was laid to rest in a corner plot in the Heavenly Mountain Cemetery. He was once quoted as saying, 'Every moment of my life was happy, every experience was heavenly', so that is what is written on his tombstone.

On the day that her husband was laid to rest, Abby sat alone at his grave-site, long after the other friends and relatives had gone. She caressed his marbled headstone with her hand and closed her eyes as she prayed.

She silently thanked all those who had contributed to his being on Earth with her. She thanked each and every one of them for everything that the two of them did and were able to share together. She then thanked the heavens and other elements for a very happy life.

Brenner watched his dear wife for a few minutes from above, and then blew her a kiss from his open hand.

Abby felt an icy tingle against her left cheek and instantly knew that it was from her beloved. She smiled as she realized that Brenner had finally gone to be with his family, and the others that had gone before him.

Brenner hated leaving Abby, but he knew that it was time. He watched his weeping wife as she stood up and dusted herself off. He closed his eyes tightly and lovingly wished her well, and then like a quick breeze he was gone. He gladly went on to the next life, knowing that he would see her again shortly.

Abby and Brenner Jaxon were happily reunited 2 years and 3 months later and spent eternity together, forever.

The End ✍

Who can say for certain
That you are not still here
I feel you all around me
Our memories so clear

Deep in the stillness
I can hear your voice
You had to leave, I know that
To love you was my choice

I'm ready now to be with you
Fly me up to where you are
To see you smile, for just a while
Beyond that distant star